Penny Appleton

Love at the
Summerfield Stables

A SUMMERFIELD VILLAGE
SWEET ROMANCE

Love at the Summerfield Stables
Copyright © Penny Appleton (2019). All rights reserved.
www.PennyAppleton.com

ISBN: 978-1-912105-20-5

For any inquiries regarding this book,
please contact the rights team at Curl Up Press:
www.curluppress.com/contact

Cover and Interior Design: JD Smith Design

www.CurlUpPress.com

Printed by Amazon KDP Print

For my much-loved daughter, Joanna,
extraordinary mentor and friend.

Chapter 1

One is a perfect number, unless you wish it were two. Living in the country, eligible guys were few, and her 31st birthday celebration had been with girlfriends, most of whom were divorced. Driving along the lane, Clair Williams had been thinking about the happy marriage of her grandparents, Ted and May, but a long-lasting love with a family of her own seemed to have passed her by.

Clair parked the old, green *Summerfield Stables* Jeep by St. Peter's church and switched off romantic thoughts with the engine. She leaned over into the back seat to pat a brown-and-white Springer spaniel and retrieved the potted lavender plant next to him. "Stay, Jossie."

Ted Williams, her grandfather, struggled from the passenger seat while she tried not to watch. He battled arthritis every day but was quickly irritated if she tried to help. Every Sunday afternoon they visited Grandma May, now at rest in St. Peter's churchyard.

Ted was a lean, old countryman with a kind face, much creased by wind and sun. He did not wear Sunday best to visit May, "She wouldn't recognize me, would she?" Ready for work on Monday, he wore clean, brown corduroy pants, a faded-green polo shirt, and solid boots. Warm against the cold wind, he had on his favorite tweed jacket. Ted walked down the path toward the church, leaning on a blackthorn cane he'd carved for his father many years before. His abundant white hair was neatly cut and parted on one side, as it had been from boyhood.

Clair shut the driver's door and Jossie jumped over onto the front seat. His tail wagged energetically, then slowly, until finally, it stopped altogether. He sat down to wait for their return.

A gust of wind, high in the beech trees above them, sent leaves like gold coins spiraling down. Clair caught up with Ted and pulled off her blue *Summerfield Stables* baseball cap to jump and catch one. "Ha! Good luck ahead!"

Clair's Sunday working outfit was warm as well, faded jeans with thermals underneath, a baggy blue sweater, and tall gumboots. Her caramel-brown eyes smiled easily; and now she shook leaves from her short, blond curls as they walked past the entrance to the beautiful old building, but the decorative iron gates across the porch were chained shut. A notice board directed worshippers to nearby parishes and Ted grunted, "They had another break-in."

St. Peter's, Church of England, had been built in the fourteenth century by the Duke of that time. He had owned all the land thereabouts and erected stone cottages for his workers. Many were still lived in today, some roofed with straw thatch and others with potlatch tiles. The same enlightened Duke allowed one of his fields to be used for recreation. It could be used in summer but often flooded in winter; over time the group of houses became known as Summerfield village. It was a pretty village with a pub called 'The Potlatch,' a few small shops, and a Farmer's Market on Wednesdays and Saturdays. Many people now commuted to work in Oxford, but there were some old families who had lived there for generations.

In the graveyard, Clair and Ted walked past old headstones that leaned at crazy angles in the long grass. Clair's grandparents, Ted and May, had both grown up in Summerfield, and were baptized, confirmed and married at St. Peter's. As a teenager,

Clair and her friend Lizzie had attended services, but over time, the congregation had dwindled away.

The area of grass around May's grave was neatly mown and the headstones were more modern. A marble angel on a large, granite base seemed to watch over them. Ted and Clair had planted many of May's favorite flowering plants around her headstone and Ted now sat down on a bench with her name and life dates carved into it. Leaning forward, he looked closely at the carved words on the headstone, as he did every week. "I fell in love with May the moment we met. Sixty years went by so fast. Every young fella in Summerfield was after her. I didn't think I was smart enough, but May chose me."

Clair sat down next to him and took his hand as Ted looked at her and smiled. "You have May's eyes, and I hear her when you giggle. She was Her Ladyship's best parlor maid, you know; served tea in the drawing room and everything."

Clair did know, because he'd told her many times before. But life was busy, and they didn't get much time to talk, so she tried hard not to be impatient. Ted sometimes spoke of wanting to follow May, yet he hung on. Clair knew it was because of her because, when he died, she would be alone.

Her father, 'Young Ted,' had been the only

child of Ted and May. He'd left Summerfield to study engineering, got married, and they had two children. Clair had been born in the city, but from an early age, she was horse crazy. Ted told her, "You're a throwback to my grandfather; you have his magic touch with horses."

Clair spent every possible vacation at Summerfield Stables, but came to live with her grandparents permanently in the year she was thirteen. She'd come early that winter break, as soon as school was finished. She waited eagerly with Ted and May for her family to arrive for the Christmas holiday. But instead of them, a police car pulled into the yard. Her mother, father, and Owen, her young brother, had been killed in a motorway accident. The hand Clair held onto now had been her lifeline.

Ted and his father and grandfather, the Williams men, had all served successions of the Duke's family caring for their farming, hunting, and carriage horses. They'd all started out as grooms and risen to be coachmen. Then each was recognized as being exceptional with horses and promoted to Head Coachman. But by 1918, not only millions of people, but eight million horses had been killed in World War I. Tractors and automobiles were being developed, and the last of the Duke's carriages was sold after Ted retired. When Clair qualified as a riding instructor, he helped her build her small equestrian business at Summerfield Stables.

Clair knelt beside the grave to plant the small lavender bush. She deposited the plastic pot in a bin and put her cap back on. "Come on Granddad, it's time to go. We've got ponies to feed, people to see, and chores to do."

She pulled Ted to his feet and soon they were walking arm in arm to the Jeep. Clair breathed deeply. She could smell yew trees, new-mown grass and Ted's old jacket, which had a comforting smell, like a hug from her childhood. She loved that he could produce so many things from its pockets, like hoof picks, apples, and useful pieces of string. Ahead of them, Jossie barked a welcome. "I forgot to mention, people in the village are asking, 'Isn't it your birthday soon? How old are you this year, and are we having a birthday party?'"

Ted snorted, "I don't want another party. We had one for my 80th birthday, and it's too sad without May. Don't you remind them of the date or how old I am! I'm as old as me tongue, and a bit older than me teeth."

Ted usually laughed when he trotted out one of his old country sayings. Today, he seemed distracted as he climbed laboriously into the driver's seat. The Jeep had *Summerfield Stables* painted on both sides and was their work vehicle. Right now, it was full of hay. Ted drove the next half mile then Clair jumped out, keyed in the code and swung open the big 5-bar gate. He drove through and down to a group of ponies waiting at the feed rack.

Clair shut the gate again and lifted her face to the late afternoon sun. Wind rustled the treetops of Potlatch Wood and there was the soft '*boo-boo, boo-boo*' call of wood doves. High above her, the blue silk sky was crisscrossed with white jet trails from Heathrow Airport.

Where were all those people going?

Clair loved her life in Summerfield and felt no desire to fly away. The beautiful Oxford countryside surrounded them; they had good land with water and shady woods on either side. The only drawback this year had been a long, scorching summer with little rain. The grass was parched and yellowing.

Jossie scooted past, nose down on the scent of rabbits, and Clair joined Ted, to move hay from the Jeep to the racks. "It's bad news to be feeding them this early, but the grass has no nutrition. At least we kept the top fields, and the feed bills will be less this year."

Ted mopped his hot face with a neckerchief but did not reply. Clair regretted her thoughtless words.

They'd disagreed over Cilla Bartlett-Brown keeping her mares on those fields.

Several generations of the Bartlett-Brown family had lived at the Manor House in Summerfield village. As boys, Ted Williams and George Bartlett-Brown had built dens in the woods together. But Ted was the son of the Duke's coachman. As adults they had moved in different social circles. At some point, after he'd become Sir George Bartlett-Brown, George persuaded Ted to give his daughter, Cilla, the use of two big fields for her horses. When Clair started a program called 'Riding with Challenges,' her team agreed that, since they were a charity, Cilla needed now to pay for the grazing. But she was insulted. "It's custom and practice for Bartlett-Browns to use these fields. I shall take legal action."

Clair had checked before she spoke with Cilla, that Summerfield Stables had no contract with the Bartlett-Browns. Now, she changed the subject. "Shame we don't own that bottom piece of land."

Bonnie, their Exmoor pony, leaned through the rails of the bottom fence to snatch at waving stems of luscious grass. In contrast to their dry grass, the wide, marshy area between the fence and the wall of the Duke's Estate was a vibrant green. Ted shut the back door of the Jeep. "No good if we did. The stream that floods the summer field runs under there. The Duke lost some valuable heifers when they died in the mud, so he had it fenced off. It's best left as it is."

It was September 1st. Schools and the Summerfield Stables would reopen the following day; and like an anxious mother, Clair checked on the ponies' coats and shoes. She called to Bonnie and she cantered over to nuzzle at pockets with an oat-colored nose. She was a pretty pony and a great favorite with the children. "Sorry girl, no treats until tomorrow."

Suddenly Clair's head shot up, as startled as the ponies. She and Ted turned toward the sound, just as there was another crack of gunshot. A black Labrador dog burst from the undergrowth at the top of the track and came racing down to meet them. Two men followed him out of the woods, laughing together, guns cracked open in the crooks of their arms.

"Kyle Sanders? What is he doing shooting here? Could you bring the Jeep, please, Granddad?"

Clair walked rapidly up the track. In high school Kyle had been a darkly handsome boy among a bunch of spotty ones and she'd been attracted to him. He'd trained as a farrier and Clair had met him again after school, when he came to shoe their horses. They dated for a short time, but she soon realized that they had little in common but horses.

Clair found his attitude towards women particularly objectionable and stopped seeing him. But Kyle was not accustomed to rejection and "bad-mouthed" her to people in the village. As she neared the men now, Clair remembered that Lizzie had never liked him. The only good thing Clair could say was that Kyle had turned her lunatic Labrador, Jester, into an excellent hunting dog.

"Hi, Clair. D'you remember Gary Kidd? From a couple of years ahead of us in high school?"

Kyle was now a big, stocky man, dressed in well-worn country clothes and boots. She did not recall ever meeting the man with him. He had ash-blond hair with sharp features. He was dressed in new, expensive shooting gear, and she could smell his cologne on the breeze. Clair stepped back involuntarily–it seemed out of place in a field. She looked into small, hard eyes that didn't seem to blink, and the back of her neck prickled. "Hi. But why are you shooting on our land? Kyle, you know very well that our ponies need to be calm in order to carry disabled children."

Gary looked her up and down with a look of disdain, as if she was some scruffy farm worker. Only the baseball cap with the *Stables* logo on it gave her authority to challenge them. "It's lease-hold land; you don't own it. An ancient footpath runs through here and we have the right to walk it."

Clair narrowed her eyes. Who was this guy?

"Summerfield Stables and its land have been a wildlife sanctuary for over sixty years. You may walk on the path, but shooting is not allowed."

Ted drove up next to them, his arm along the open window of the Jeep. "A good day to you both."

"Afternoon, Ted. This is my friend, Gary Kidd. Gary, Ted Williams."

They nodded to each other, just as Gary's mobile phone burst into a loud rap. He handed his gun to Kyle, "Yeah?"

Clair ground her teeth and was about to make an acid comment when he clicked it off again. He took his gun back and Kyle grinned awkwardly. "It's Sunday afternoon, I thought you'd be glued to the European soccer on TV."

Ted looked him straight in the eye. "I'm heading back now to watch the qualifiers. But whether we're here or not, I'll thank you not to shoot on our property again."

Clair grabbed Jossie as the dogs raced past. She loaded him into the Jeep and heard Gary laugh. "You never know, it might not be theirs for much longer."

Her brow furrowed as she followed the Jeep bumping back up the track. She locked the gate and watched the two men. Kyle pointed this way and that, then whistled for Jester and they disappeared into the woods. There were no more shots and the ponies fed quietly. Clair pushed Jossie into the back and climbed into the passenger seat. "What was that all about? I've never seen that creepy guy before."

Ted did not start the engine again but passed her the crumpled sheet of paper he had been holding. "I'm sorry, dear. I've tried to deal with this, but it's gone out of my control."

Clair smoothed out a letter with the Duke's crest at the top and the address of his Land Agent. She scanned the contents. Then, incredulous, she read it again. "I don't understand. The lease to Summerfield Stables is now terminated and they're going to hold an open auction? But I thought...I thought the lease was ours for life?"

"I thought so too." Ted rubbed his face. "I was Head Coachman, like my father and grandfather before me. The old Duke made May and me a gift of the lease at our wedding. It was in recognition of devoted service by generations of our family. But he's dead–and the Bartlett-Browns are famous for seeking revenge."

"But what have the Bartlett-Browns to do with this?"

"Cilla's hired a lawyer. She intends to take the Stables away from us."

Chapter 2

A power mower chugged steadily up and down outside the Manor House, cutting close parallel lines on the immaculate lawn. David Bartlett-Brown fought to wake through the fog of sleeping tablets, as the sound triggered his worst nightmare.

A military helicopter rose above soft, green English fields and he was in it. There seemed to be no time gap before it landed in the Afghan desert. The sky was a hot blue with not a cloud in sight. David plucked at the bedcovers but could not get his eyes to open. Pack slung over his shoulder, he walked between fuel dumps, toward the temporary buildings. Then Kate appeared through a shimmering mirage of white tents. Her brown hair was pinned up beneath a green beret and she wore khaki military fatigues. A big 'sniffer dog' paced beside her and she smiled in delight to see David. He tried to stop the video in his head. But she saluted smartly and put the dog into a 'down' position.

A door opened nearby, and the Afghani College principal came out with his staff. He smiled, his arm extended to shake hands, when suddenly, the dog barked an alarm and sprang to his feet.

There was a bright flash and David catapulted into the air. He felt no pain but in slow motion, he began to fall.

Down, down, down, into a haze of sand and blood. "No!"

* * *

David sat up and forced his gritty eyes open. He was in Summerfield. But it was too fast. A monster wave of vertigo broke in his gut and swirled like a whirlpool in his brain. Desperately, he bent forward, wrapped both arms around his stomach, and focused on the strip of light between the drapes.

Long, deep breaths now...in-ha-lation. Hold it... ex-ha-lation.

There was a brisk rap at the door and his sister, Cilla, swept in with a tray of breakfast. "Good morning–another beautiful day."

She put the tray on a side table and flung open the drapes. "Cilla…no!" David threw his arm across his face and she turned in surprise as the light hit him.

* * *

Her brother huddled into the pillow, his face as white as the sheets. She was forty-four years old; David was now forty and they had not lived under the same roof for many years. Now she studied him. His dark hair was military short, greying at the sides and in the stubble on his chin. Faint blast marks on his face did not make him less handsome than before the incident in Afghanistan.

Her memory circled back to when she was eight years old and David only four years. Their father, George, had divorced his second wife, Nancy, their mother. She was an American and his top legal team won custody, to keep her and David in the UK. George had then denied their mother access. Desperately unhappy, Nancy returned to California, but their father rarely came back to the Manor House after that. He hired nannies and housekeepers and she had taken care of David when they travelled to either parent for vacations. When he was eleven, David was sent to the military academy attended by his grandfather and Cilla went to finishing school in Switzerland.

But now David was home again.

* * *

Squinting through half-closed eyes, David knew Cilla was assessing him. "Thanks for breakfast. I'll shower first. Are you going riding?"

She was dressed in a tailored jacket, fitted black pants, and tall boots, her light-brown hair drawn back in a clip.

"Zara and I have a dressage lesson. The only nuisance is that the horses are in Woodstock."

Cilla drew soft riding gloves from her pocket. "The men will be here at eleven o'clock to install your home gym. I'll be back by then, but I need you to check everything. Do you need help getting dressed?"

"I'm good, thanks, and I'll be ready at eleven."

She paused at the door, looking back at him. "I'm glad you're here. You're our wounded hero, and I'm going to look after you from now on."

Cilla closed the door and David used the remote control to bring his hospital bed slowly to a sitting position. His room overlooked the driveway and he watched as Cilla marched out to her massive, white 4 x 4 Range Rover. She'd always been fiercely competitive, and her horses were the best of the best. An accomplished horsewoman, she now had a wall of trophies and an exclusive equestrian boutique in the village. As she drove out of the driveway between the big pillars, David remembered her marriage. It was to the son of one of Sir George's friends, but he had proved as unreliable as their father. Cilla returned to Summerfield wealthier after the divorce, but David had never heard of another relationship. In partnership with her friend Zara, she now owned brood mares and dressage horses.

Her sudden arrival seemed to have stopped his vertigo. Was that what was needed? A short, sharp shock and then power on through? But he'd get a lock put the door to the hallway today. The last thing he needed was Cilla fussing over him as if he was a kid again.

David edged cautiously from his bed and into the wheelchair, heading through to the gold and onyx bathroom. George was in his eighties and lived on his yacht in the Mediterranean. David smiled at the irony of now occupying his father's rooms. Positioning the wheelchair, he braced on his arms to slide across to the shower seat. But vertigo struck again.

Desperately, he reached out to grab the rail. But

his hand found nothing before the stump of his amputated leg hit the floor. Tears of agony burst from his eyes. Unable to hold it back any longer, David hugged the bleeding leg to his chest and wept for everything he had lost.

After a while, he forced his cold, bruised body to uncurl, bit his lower lip between his teeth, and rolled to the wheelchair. No one would come to find him, unless it was Cilla, when he didn't show up at 11:00 a.m. Using the strength in muscular arms, he hauled himself up and reached into the bathroom cabinet for wound dressings and pain pills. Above where his right knee should have been, the skin grafts bled copiously. Swallowing two painkillers with a drink of water, David applied new dressings. "Patience, that's what the medics say. Never was one of my strengths."

He'd been in the London military center for amputees, which deliberately did not have mirrors in bathrooms. Now, he looked at multiple reflections of himself. "Think you'll ever be attractive to a woman again?"

David grinned wryly at himself. "Why did I think of that now?"

Other veterans in the hospital had worse injuries than his, but he suffered from unpredictable attacks of vertigo, unable to stand up, let alone walk. His prosthetic leg waited by the door to be strapped on, but he no longer had the energy and abandoned the idea of taking a shower. Back in the chair, he wheeled into the bedroom to answer his phone.

"David? It's Jack Harris. I'm near Summerfield, just completing a visit with another veteran. Would it be convenient to come over?"

* * *

David had managed to put on underwear, a white t-shirt, and black sweatpants before there was a knock at the door. At his call, Mrs. Jessop, housekeeper at the Manor House, put her head inside the room. "You have a visitor, sir, a Major Harris."

David smiled and indicated his left foot, the sock only halfway on. "I'll be ready in five minutes. Might we have coffee in my sitting room?"

"Certainly, sir. Please ring when you're ready."

She withdrew, taking the untouched breakfast tray with her. David thought about Sarah Jessop as he conquered the sock and running shoe. He'd not met her before his return to Summerfield this time, but she'd been with Cilla for some time. Aged about fifty, with her hair in a neat grey bob and wearing a tailored black dress and formal shoes, she seemed every inch the discreet and professional housekeeper.

David tucked the right leg of his sweatpants up and under the cushion before wheeling through the interior door between bedroom and sitting room. He shut it behind him and rang the bell.

Mrs. Jessop opened the door to the hallway. "Major Jack Harris."

Jack was slightly older than David, stocky, with sandy hair and a small moustache. He wore their Regimental uniform, with a military cap in one hand and a briefcase in the other. He laid both on the coffee table before shaking hands with David. "Thanks for seeing me at such short notice."

Jack managed the Welfare Program for returning veterans in the Oxford area. David had met him once before, at the London hospital, because Jack was the officer who would sign him off to return to work. David now regretted not putting on his prosthetic leg.

Jack stared through the long windows in their carved stone mountings. "This is a wonderful place."

Close to the house a stone terrace bordered long rose gardens, with late pink blooms in neat beds. Green pastures and plowed furrows stretched between the Manor House and the horizon. "Thank you." David spun his wheels across the smooth oak boards, to a fireplace full of autumn leaves and yellow chrysanthemums. "My sister had these ground floor rooms converted for me, to make it easier for the wheelchair. Please come and sit down."

There was a tap at the door and Mrs. Jessop brought in coffee with homemade cookies. Jack sat in a huge comfy couch and looked around as she served them and left the room quietly. Two big couches were upholstered in traditional floral fabric and faced each other across the elegant coffee table. A big-screen TV had been mounted discreetly between floor-to-ceiling bookcases that were filled with leather-bound books.

"You have an excellent setup here. It will help you transition more easily to civilian life."

David stiffened and stared at him over the rim of his coffee cup, "This is only a temporary arrangement. If I thought this was going to be my life from now on, I'd rather have died with that suicide bomber. I had a career that I loved, and I want to go back to the Regiment. Can you help me with that?"

Jack sipped his coffee reflectively and nodded at him. "Okay, if that's your goal, we need to get you mixing with people again as soon as possible." He put the cup down on its saucer and took a tablet computer from his briefcase. "We have a

Support Group in Oxford, and there's a part-time job opportunity at the Business College. It would be mentally stimulating and get you back into the routine of work."

Jack knew that David had been an Army management consultant and he turned the computer to share the screen of information about the college. "They need tutors on a management module, one afternoon and evening per week."

David read the details. "I can do that okay, but my priority is to get this balance issue fixed. I must find a way to counteract the vertigo. One of those bull-riding machines might help."

Jack was typing, then he looked up and grinned. "Even better than that, your physical therapist said that riding a horse could help. You've ridden before so I already called the head office of a program called 'Riding with Challenges.' You're in luck; the only accredited instructor between here and London works at Summerfield Stables. You are correct about conquering the vertigo. Until you've done that, I can't sign you off as fit to return to work."

Chapter 3

At 6:30 a.m. the next morning, it was just light at Stables Cottage. There was a freezing nip to the air when Clair let Jossie into the yard and opened the little door of the chicken coop. Clucks were heard and flurries of feathers flew as the hens rushed over to the shallow food trough. Clair's misty breath rose in clouds as she fed them.

May had known all her hens by name. But they were long gone, and it was Ted's job to look after the chickens now; to feed them, collect the eggs, and repair wire mesh to keep the foxes out. But Ted had not risen this morning with his alarm. Not hearing him moving about, Clair tapped lightly on the door. "Granddad? Are you okay?"

He was obviously still in bed. "Could you feed the chickens please, dear? I'll get up in a while, but

I'm not coming to the staff meeting. I'll walk Jossie to St. Peter's, and talk things over with May."

After May died, Ted had moved downstairs and made the small sitting room into his bedroom and den. "We only use that room at Christmas. It's less strain on my legs than climbing those stairs."

Clair's bedroom was up there, and the cottage stairs were indeed steep and narrow. But she knew he could no longer rest in the bed he'd shared with May all their married life. Ted and Clair spent most time together in the big kitchen, close to the warm stove and fond memories of May's cooking. Ted did not cook much, and Clair was less than enthusiastic about doing it. It was not a natural talent for her.

Now she locked the wire door to the chicken run and put Jossie back into the kitchen to wait for Ted. Her fitted blue jeans and short, jodhpur boots were suitable for teaching in the arena today. She pulled the quilted jacket tighter around her and pushed her hands deeper into the pockets. After a night worrying about the Land Agent's letter, Clair looked around her with new eyes, aware that they could lose it all.

The Stables building formed three sides of a square around a big cobbled yard; the fourth side was an arch, with '1743' carved at the top. Constructed in the same sand-colored stone as the

Duke's Mansion, it had a roof of potlatch tiles like many old properties in Summerfield. Potlatches were round stone boulders that were once scattered all over the landscape.

When she was young, Clair had tried to lift the one like a stone soccer ball that they used as a doorstop for the front door. Ted had roared with laughter. "That's been there for a hundred years and it's too heavy for you. A long time ago, before the Romans invaded England, glaciers pushed rocks down the hills and dumped them around here, totally round and smooth. Heavy frost split them into slices and people used them to make roof tiles."

"Is that why our pub is called 'The Potlatch'?"

He'd patted his observant granddaughter on the back. "Well spotted. That's right, but it's rare to find a potlatch around here nowadays; they've all been collected."

Clair turned at the gate to the yard and looked back at Stables Cottage. The rising sun slanted across pink-tinted walls and Clair's eyes softened. It was older than the yard buildings and for two hundred years had been home to Head Coachmen and their families. The cottage was a low, rectangular building with a thatched roof of tightly packed straw. The blond straw was covered with mesh, to stop the birds from stealing it for nests. Ted grew spinach and herbs in raised vegetable beds, but May had planted the flower borders. The lavender bushes by the gate had grown to be giants and wallflowers of every color still bloomed. But four cars were already in the parking lot, so she needed to get going. Clair shut the gate behind her and jogged across the yard. Under the elegant arch, she passed the big, blue signboard.

Welcome to Summerfield Stables
Proprietors: Ted and Clair Williams

Inside the horse barn there was the stamp of hooves and a cheerful shout, "Get over, Bella!" A radio played from the tack room and Clair smiled, determined to push aside her worries and welcome everyone back. The pony stalls were along the left arm of the square. Several volunteers were mucking out the stalls and there was the astringent smell of wet straw in the air.

"Morning, Clair."

"Good morning to everyone, and thanks for being here so early. Day One of the new school year! I can't wait to see our students again."

Clair had been a riding instructor for several years. Then she trained with the charity, 'Riding with Challenges' and started a branch at Summerfield

Stables. Its mission was to support people with injuries or disability to heal through riding horses– and Clair was passionate about it. Her eyes were sparkling now. She had a great team of people working with her, doing important work in a place that she loved. It didn't come much better than that.

Ponies–grey, black, and bay–looked over the half-doors of their stalls, and Clair stroked noses as she walked down the line. Eyes alert, ears flickering this way and that, there was an air of expectancy. She paused by the entrance to the indoor arena. All was ready for the first lesson, inside the huge barn that had been Ted and May's amazing gift for her twenty-first birthday. She'd unwrapped the plans on the kitchen table along with her other gifts and cards and was stunned. "This is unbelievable!"

May had beamed with happiness. "We had some savings put by. Ted had it designed for special-needs students and we got planning permission to connect it to the horse barn." Ted was as excited as Clair. "That means easy access for the horses and riders. You can give lessons in the arena when it's cold and wet outside."

Once the building was completed, Clair could offer riding and jumping lessons for able-bodied students and now had forty youngsters in the 'Riding with Challenges' program.

Robert Kennet, Stables Manager, came out of the feed store. "Morning, Clair." In his late forties, he was a big man with greying hair in a buzz cut. Robert had been an officer in the UK Mounted Police. He and Winston, his big dapple-grey horse, had been trapped and injured by a drunken crowd at a soccer match. He'd been forced to retire early and trauma had strained his marriage. Robert's wife and two sons still lived in Birmingham. He had accepted the Summerfield Stables job because it had a custodian apartment and Winston came with him as part of the deal. For the start of the new year, he wore a long-sleeved navy *Summerfield Stables* polo shirt, with a black quilted vest, and boots over his denim jeans. His limp was barely noticeable, but Clair knew he suffered with back pain.

"Winston's cast a shoe, but the farrier's here to trim pony feet. He says he'll shoe him after that."

Clair tensed, then remembered that Kyle was no longer their farrier. "Great, he's not needed until tonight, for the able-bodied lessons."

Clair stroked Winston's Roman nose and the big grey horse blew gently through his nostrils. He and the other horses were housed on the opposite side of the stables from the ponies and had bigger stalls. Clair rotated supervision duties with Robert, and he'd been to visit his family in Birmingham the previous day. He did not know about the devastating news she would need to share at the morning meeting. Stephanie Partridge, Clair's other salaried member of staff, followed Robert out of the tack room, a saddle over each arm.

"Morning, Steph." Clair took a saddle from her and swung it to rest on the half-door of Blackbird's stall.

"Hi Clair, busy morning ahead! We've got lots of new volunteers to train today."

She and Steph were the same age and had been in the same grade at high school. They'd travelled on the school bus to Banbury every day with Lizzie Martin. The morning journeys were for completing homework, but in the afternoons, they'd giggled happily together all the way home. Lizzie was now married to Harry and lived in Scotland, and Clair appreciated having one close friend still in Summerfield.

Steph was in jeans and a blue *Stables* polo shirt. She managed everything to do with volunteers at the Stables–their recruitment, background checks, and daily schedules. A head shorter than Clair, her long, blond ponytail was pulled through the back of her cap and she looked like a teenager. But, she'd become pregnant at sixteen by her village boyfriend and had to leave high school. They married, but their baby was born damaged. The young father left Summerfield, unable to cope with a disabled child, so Steph was a single mother, working to support him. Their son, Nick, was now twelve.

Glancing at her watch, Clair blew out a long breath and turned toward the training room. As she walked, Clair bounced a little on her toes with nerves. She missed Ted; and she needed to gain control of her heart rate before the meeting. Robert was in front of them. "I'll get the coffee."

Steph stepped in to walk beside her. "Did you hear anything from Lizzie over the summer?"

"A couple of times, but she and Harry have art exhibitions running, and now she's studying again. Before the meeting, I wanted to ask you, do you know a guy named Gary Kidd?"

"I know *of* him. His family owns chicken farms, 'Kidd's Chunky Chicks.' Gary got teased at school and was called 'the chicken-shack Kidd.' Why do you ask?"

Clair paused at the door to the training room, "Granddad and I met him yesterday, with his new best buddy, Kyle. They were shooting rabbits in Potlatch Wood."

Steph knew of Clair's difficulties with Kyle. "Uh-oh, that sounds ominous. Is he still angry because you changed farriers?"

"I don't know if that's the reason, but he's still telling people I'm playing hard to get. He's taken to parking at the top of our lane to walk Jester in Potlatch Wood and it feels like he's stalking me."

Clair held a quick 'get-together' with her team every working day at 7:30 a.m., before the students arrived at 8:30 a.m. The Training Room was a part of the arena and built onto Reception, with the custodian apartment above. It was bright and airy, big enough for meetings and workshops. One set of big windows looked onto the parking lot; three smaller ones overlooked the arena. She pushed the door open. "Morning, Sid, morning, Patricia. Welcome back!"

Clair took the mug of coffee Robert held out and smiled her thanks. She sat down at one of the big tables, next to Sid.

Sid Green was Lizzie's uncle, a retired accountant and their volunteer financial advisor. Clair was very fond of him and of Lizzie's aunt, Viv. They lived in Oxford and were long-time friends of Ted and May. Sid was a quiet man, rotund in a comfortable sort of way, and always dressed for work in a baggy tweed suit. Three days a week, Patricia Anderson was their gem of a volunteer Office Manager. She'd also joined the team through the 'Lizzie connection.' She'd retired and moved to Summerfield but previously worked with Viv as an administrator at an Oxford college. Patricia had short, white hair and a lovely smile; at age sixty-six, she had the energy of a much younger woman.

Clair took photocopies of the letter from a big envelope and passed them out. "There's no time for catch-ups or operational stuff today, guys, this is urgent."

Sid indicated the empty chair next to him. "We're not waiting for Ted?"

"Sadly, no. He only showed me this letter yesterday and he's upset he couldn't sort it out. But if Cilla Bartlett-Brown is behind this, then it's my fault, not his."

Steph had read the letter now and exploded, "Don't blame yourself–it's her fault! She refused to pay her bills and you had no choice but to evict her. Her mares needed to come off the hayfields or we'd be short of winter fodder. But why is she doing this now?"

Patricia leaned forward. "Sarah Jessop, her housekeeper, sings in the same choir as me. We go for coffee afterwards and she told me quietly that Cilla was madder than a hornet at having to move her horses to Woodstock. She's the Queen of Summerfield to all her friends, and she lost face."

Sid smoothed back thinning white hair, obviously

uncomfortable. "I'm sorry I couldn't say anything, Clair, but Ted made me promise."

Clair's cheeks reddened. "Don't worry, it happens all the time. He thinks I'm still thirteen, with braces on my teeth. But I'm struggling with the implications of this, so I'll read the last part out loud. Then we need to discuss what we're going to do."

She took a sip of coffee to lubricate her throat.

"The Lease to Summerfield Stables and Land, claimed to be given as a marital gift to Edward and May Williams by the late Duke, is declared null and void. After an extensive Legal search, Ogilvy and Ogilvy find no evidence to support this claim.

We hereby give notice, as of December 31st, any historical arrangement of Edward Williams with the Duke's Estate is terminated. On instructions from the Duke, there will be an Open Auction of said Lease, to be held at Summerfield Stables, at 1:00 p.m. on January 3rd."

Chapter 4

Patricia looked up from the letter, "This is dreadful."

Clair pulled one knee up to her chest and hugged it. "My thoughts exactly. Can you tell us more, Sid? Granddad said to ask if you found anything useful in the Oxford Records Office? There's never been any doubt in his mind that the Duke gave the Williams family the lease for life. I'm the last of the family and we've built a business on that."

Sid pulled a folder from his old briefcase and laid it opened it on the table. "Everyone knows that Ted was a favorite of the old Duke, but if there was ever a Deed of Gift, it's gone."

"You didn't find any documentation at all?"

"Sixty years ago, the Duke's word was law and benefits like this were given to long-serving members of his staff. I accessed the correct file in the

Public Records office, but either there is nothing, or someone else was there before me. There's a thick file of other documents from that time and you can borrow them to photocopy. I'm not suggesting anything, but it is possible to take a document and not return it."

He cleared his throat, "The Land Agent, Quentin Ogilvy, claims that since the old Duke died, the young one has commissioned him to examine all leases. But he could be using Cilla's complaint, to better establish himself."

Steph snorted. "That sounds more like it. Quentin Ogilvy is known in the village as a slippery customer."

Robert spoke rarely in meetings but now he spoke up. "Could we raise enough money to bid for the lease at auction? If we can't dispute it, can we win it back?"

Clair dropped her knee and leaned forward. "I thought about that too. But we have less than three months to raise the money. How much do leases like this sell for?"

They all looked at Sid and he shrugged. "Summerfield is a designated Area of Outstanding Natural Beauty, so industrial or residential companies are not allowed to bid. The local dairy farmers will be interested, but the amount paid always depends on the competition."

Clair glanced up at the clock. "We can't be late, so we need to decide. Between now and Christmas, do we work at closing the Stables and finding homes for the horses and ponies? Or put our energy into raising money? Do you want to think about it today and vote at tomorrow's meeting?"

Steph looked around at the others. "I'm ready to vote now. What do you think?"

Everyone nodded.

"Okay, all in favor of closing the business?"

No hands.

"All in favor of raising money and winning at the auction?"

Everyone raised a hand and Clair grinned. "Okay, we fight! Please tell everyone, because we need them all involved–parents, students, and volunteers. Ask for fund-raising ideas and bring them tomorrow."

Robert, Steph, and Sid stood up and carried their mugs into the kitchen, discussing the letter. "Clair, could you just look at this urgent email before you go?"

Patricia angled her screen to show Clair the message. "Major Harris is a military rehabilitation officer, seeking help for an amputee. The injured officer suffers with severe vertigo and they can pay full fees, which would help the auction fund."

Clair screwed up her face and turned for the door. "Sorry, we're doing the induction of new volunteers in this lesson and I need to hurry. Honestly, I don't have the necessary experience to work with this man. The London center does, so please could you refer Major Harris to them?"

"He contacted me after the London office because the officer has just come home to Summerfield. He can't travel much, because of the vertigo. Could we just do a brief assessment? I hate to turn him away and you have an hour free at the end of this morning."

Clair laughed. "Okay! You sound determined to make this happen, so set it up. But I haven't heard anything about a veteran coming home. Who is it?"

"David Bartlett-Brown, Cilla's younger brother."

* * *

Patricia had only lived in Summerfield a short time and did not know village history. As Clair hurried down the corridor, her mind flashed back to the Christmas vacation when she was fourteen. It had begun with low skies, full of soft snowflakes. That night there was a heavy fall, and everyone awoke to huge drifts and magic trees. All the village kids gathered on the market square, just as the Bartlett-Browns came out of their driveway. There was a big snowball fight! But then a truce was called and the steep hill behind Potlatch Wood came alive. Everyone was zooming down and hauling sleds back up the hill to go again.

David and Cilla had got the aluminum hood from a motorcycle sidecar from somewhere. Turned upside down, the curled lip at the front made it a superfast sled! They sat side by side and took off down the hill, laughing. David shouting, "Look out, here comes the Bartlett-Brown bomber!"

Between the two fields was a gateway. They whizzed through it, and on down to the bottom of the hill. Then it was Clair and Lizzie's turn, on Ted's old wooden sled. They shrieked as it gathered speed, snow flying up all around them. But the sled was hard to steer, and they skidded through the gateway. Clair fell off, rolling and rolling; until her head slammed into a gate post.

Anxious faces loomed above her when she opened her eyes and David Bartlett-Brown sat beside her, holding her hand. "You need to stay still. There's a huge lump on your forehead, and someone's called the ambulance."

Clair was dazed but comforted by his voice and

warm under the coat he had laid over her. After two days in the hospital with a mild concussion, she was sent home. But by then David had returned to his military academy and they had not met since. He was injured; perhaps she could help him now?

Clair pressed the pad to open the automatic doors and joined Steph in the arena. "Good morning, everyone! It's great to see you again."

Fitted with safety helmets, three students waited on the loading ramp in their wheelchairs. Across the sandy floor came their ponies–Tosca, a silvery-grey Welsh Mountain mare; Bonnie, the Exmoor pony; and Robin, a chestnut gelding. Stables Gold Badge volunteers led each pony, and Silver Badge holders walked on either side to support the riders. Staff and volunteers were all asked to wear picture badges with their first names on them. Clair waved to her students and adjusted her badge before jumping onto the ramp to greet the small group of people walking behind the ponies.

"Hi! And a warm welcome to our new volunteers."

All the caregivers applauded enthusiastically.

"I'm Clair Williams and I'm proud to show you the arena where we do most of our work."

She swept an arm around, indicating the huge space, with its tiered seating along one side. "Today, we're also using a state-of-the-art hoist, to help mount and dismount our students more easily."

Clair squatted down by the first wheelchair, "Good morning, Emily."

A tiny girl looked up at Clair from beneath her special helmet, blue eyes sparkling with excitement.

"Emily is eight and has been riding with us for a year. She has kindly agreed to be our model today."

Emily's mum positioned the wheelchair and Steph brought Tosca close to the platform as Clair unlocked the hoist.

"Tosca is twelve years old and exactly the sort of versatile pony we need for our work. Three people coordinate to move a student safely from wheelchair to saddle, and then vice versa. We always ask a student's permission before we touch them. Em, is it okay for me to put the harness around you?"

The little girl nodded, and Clair carefully strapped her in, supporting her legs in the strong, green net underneath. Using the motorized controls, she lifted Emily into the air and slowly swung the extending arm across Tosca's back. Two Silver Badge volunteers asked permission to touch her legs and Emily was lowered into her customized saddle, feet secured into special stirrups.

She smiled and patted her pony's neck. "Hello, Tosca."

Then Clair worked with the new volunteers to

mount the other students. "Well done! It's warm and sunny outside, so we'll go along the top track around Potlatch Wood and do some exercises, to stretch our muscles after the long vacation."

Steph led the way with Tosca and Emily, and the group followed, through the big doors exiting the arena and into the woods.

* * *

In the training room after the ride, Clair led a lively question-and-answer session about the 'Riding with Challenges' program.

"Is four the usual number of students in a class?"

"I take a maximum of four challenged students in a group, but I also do one-on-one work, depending on need. We are lucky to have several part-time instructors who help with the able-bodied classes."

She smiled. "Let's finish now, and I'll hand you back to Steph for the practical stable work. But I want to thank you so much for choosing us. We know that many other worthy causes are also looking for volunteers, but our challenged students need you so much. They often spend their whole lives in wheelchairs; on a pony they are in the air, level with you or above. You set them free to be a princess, a knight, or a Paralympian. You make them a star, and it makes the hard work worthwhile."

Patricia put her head around the door. "Your new client is here."

A new, white disability van had arrived in the parking lot. Clair looked down and fastened a button on her shirt. "We've been so busy I'd forgotten he was coming."

She watched from the window as the driver unloaded a wheelchair. The man in it had dark hair and a stubbly beard. His right leg was missing below the knee and he waved the driver away impatiently. "I wheel myself."

* * *

David knew his face was flushed and he was near to exploding. It was embarrassing enough to be loaded into a disability van and strapped in; but on the way through Summerfield, teenagers lounging on the War Memorial steps had craned their necks to see who was in the van. David had stared back with narrowed eyes, his damaged leg throbbing. Now, he turned the wheelchair and accelerated along the path, pushing the wheels forcefully around with gloved hands.

The door to the building opened and a young

woman came out. She was tall and slim, had short, curly hair and a warm smile. On the bright blue shirt, there was a picture name badge: *Clair Williams.*

David was startled. He stopped pushing the wheels as he remembered a snowball fight against the village kids. An attractive teenage girl in a red coat and beanie hat had thrown a snowball that hit him between his collar and ear. She'd shouted with laughter, then covered her mouth with her hand as he grabbed at the snow sliding down inside his shirt.

This was the same girl.

She could not be his instructor; he could not face her pity.

Too late. She had reached him, and an older man was close behind.

"Captain Bartlett-Brown? I don't know if you remember me … I'm Clair Williams, and this is Robert Kennet, our Stables Manager."

David stared up at them. He loathed being at waist height and his voice came out aggressively.

"I remember who you are. I do not use Bartlett-Brown; just Brown. And only military personnel address me as 'Captain.'"

In the silence, Robert coughed politely, "Clair, shall I check Blackbird and bring him into the arena?"

She stood up straight and lifted her chin. "Thanks. I'll show Mr. Brown around; then we'll try the mounting procedure."

She led along a smooth concrete path where several horses looked over half-doors. "We currently have sixteen horses and ponies. This is Winston, solid as a rock, then Bella. This empty stall belonged to Russ, my Grandfather's horse. Sadly, he's no longer with us, but you might remember him from when you lived here. He was the last of the Duke's carriage horses and quite famous."

What was she babbling on about? David moved his wheels back and forth, impatiently.

"Next to Bella is Rebel, and Robert is tacking up Blackbird for you. He's a quiet horse and we'll be doing your assessment with him today."

What was he supposed to say?

After a moment or two, she led the way along a corridor and through automatic doors onto a loading ramp. "Everything here is wheelchair friendly."

He looked around at the big arena as Clair shook out ropes and a harness, explaining the hoist contraption. Her voice shook a little, then the manager brought in the black horse, with two other women walking beside him.

"Great! We're ready. Guys, Mr. Brown is here for

his assessment. He's ridden in the past, so let's see how we get on with him in the saddle."

David held up a commanding hand. "Don't talk over me, Miss Williams. I've lost a leg, not my brain. And if you think I'm going to be hoisted in that net like a bunch of bananas, think again."

Chapter 5

David flicked the chair onto its back wheels and accelerated down the ramp. He pounded the opening pad with a clenched fist.

The doors swung open and he barreled through, shouting at the top of his voice. They could see his driver in Reception, drinking a cup of coffee. He spilled the coffee all down his front and rushed after the wheelchair.

They watched in silence as he loaded David and drove away.

* * *

"You okay?"

"Of course!" Clair laughed uncomfortably. "That was a first, wasn't it? I don't usually have such a traumatic effect on new clients."

"Don't take it too personally. I think he's still in shock. I felt like that when I had to leave the police force. One minute, I was a successful officer in control of a company of men; next minute, not in control of anything much at all." Robert patted Blackbird's glossy neck. "Come on, old fella, you're not working this session after all."

"I think I'll go and eat lunch with Granddad."

Steph and Victoria followed Robert, and Steph called back, trying to be cheerful, "See you at the fundraising meeting later."

Luckily, Ted was not at home. Clair bounded up the stairs two at a time, closed her bedroom door, and leaned her hot forehead against it. She could feel the faint indent of the sledding scar against the wood. Sighing wearily, she pulled off her boots and crawled under the throw on her bed. She had so eagerly anticipated meeting David again. She'd last seen him as a teenager, and now she saw him through the eyes of a woman. She was attracted to him again, but he'd looked at her as if she was a kindergarten teacher, playing with ponies.

What a fiasco! Clair thumped her pillow, pulled the throw tighter around her, and stared up at the clouds outside the window. Ted and May had been such good friends. Had it been like that from the start? Steph said she was old-fashioned and unrealistic. She could even hear her voice. *"You need to roll with the times, babe! A romantic partnership like Ted and May's is not possible in this day and age."* Was there nowhere a man she could love as a dear friend? Who might love her for who she was?

Clair sighed and rolled off the bed. The fundraising meeting started in twenty minutes; then she had a jumping lesson with able-bodied students. This was no time to analyze relationships. She found her phone and dialed.

"Jack Harris."

"Hi, Clair Williams, Summerfield Stables. I'm afraid we didn't get off to a good start with your client."

She spoke in her brightest PR voice, glad that he couldn't see her embarrassment.

"Hello, Clair. Yes, David's been on the phone, ranting at me. I listened for a bit, then told him the London office says you are one of their best instructors, and that he'd be lucky to work with you."

"Thanks for that."

"I can only apologize, but it's normal for returning vets to find new situations challenging. David's finding it tough, like all veterans who lose the focus of Army life. He's struggling with being an amputee, but the vertigo drives him crazy, and he's on a lot of meds."

Clair's tension lessened and she breathed a little easier. Normal, okay. Challenged in a different way than the youngsters. She had a lot to learn. Jack was still speaking. "If David wants to address his vertigo through riding, he needs to meet you halfway. Either that or wait until he's able to travel to London."

"I really would like to help. I can talk to trainers at the head office. Do you have any guidelines for amputee rehabilitation?"

"I'll send you the links now. If we can get David riding, maybe we could offer lessons to other veterans."

Clair clicked off the phone, grabbed her boots, and headed downstairs. Had Jack Harris heard that Summerfield Stables was under threat? He sounded sympathetic, and he'd be a good contact, if they could stay in business.

There was still no sign of Ted, so Clair made a sandwich. She ate it standing at the kitchen sink, looking over his vegetable patch. Probably the last thing she needed was coffee; but suddenly, she was desperate for a big mug of fresh, strong brew, something to kick-start the afternoon.

Shutting the cottage door behind her, Clair hurried down the path. Between her and the training room, Quentin Ogilvy, the Duke's Land Agent, was climbing out of his big, shiny car.

"Ah, Clair, just the person I needed to see."

Quentin was forty-something and had been considered good looking when young. He'd put on a lot of weight since then but dressed it in generously tailored suits, handmade by the same tailor as the Duke. Quentin had trained with his father in the land agency business. When Ogilvy Senior died, he became all of *Ogilvy and Ogilvy* and represented many of the landed gentry in the area. Most of his business was conducted in the bar at the Golf Club.

He held out a big brown envelope to Clair. "This is the draft flyer for the auction. If you need to change anything, you need to contact my secretary immediately. I also want a viewing date for prospective buyers. Do you have your calendar on your phone?"

Clair clenched her teeth, holding the envelope tightly. "Actually, Quentin, we're still in shock that an auction is happening at all."

He eyed her sharply, then guffawed. "Ha! No doubt about that, I'm afraid."

Quentin drummed his fingers on his car roof then stared at his ornate wedding ring, obviously thinking of other things. Clair looked at the flyer.

"I'm just going into a meeting and I'll show this to the team. Our Office Manager will get back to your

Office Manager with the information you require."

Clair was being what she called 'snotty,' but Quentin didn't seem to notice.

He looked critically around the parking lot. "When you're talking to your people, better get them to do some tidying up before the viewing." He opened his car door. "And, of course, I need to know how soon you can vacate the premises, if you are unsuccessful at the auction."

* * *

Clair exploded into the training room and Robert burst out laughing. "I was watching you out there! How is dear Quentin today?"

She made a gruesome face and passed him the envelope. "This is the flyer for the auction. He wanted a date for viewing, right then, and seeing a few wisps of straw, he suggested we tidy up! He also wants to know how soon we can move out when we lose the auction."

Steph gave her a mug of strong coffee and Patricia offered her a pretty plate with assorted muffins.

"These are for the next bake sale; tell me what you think."

Clair chose a chocolate muffin in a floral paper wrapper and gratefully sipped her coffee. "Oh, thank you, I needed this! I'll load up on caffeine and sugar while you tell me what you've come up with so far."

Sid consulted his notes. "We've discussed asking the head office to help. Robert and Steph are running a Sponsored Ride, and Patricia's coordinating the bake sales."

Clair popped another piece of muffin into her mouth. "Yum, I love this orange zest with the chocolate."

Patricia beamed, "Thanks! Is Ted joining us today?"

"Actually, I'm worried. Has anyone seen him?"

Robert looked up from reading the flyer. "I dropped him in the village earlier. He's still upset. Give him some time, and he'll come around."

Sid cleared his throat. "Then we need to get back to business. All your ideas are great, but they won't raise enough money to compete at the auction."

Everyone focused their attention on him. "Our best option, I think, is to pitch to local banks and businesses. Most have a philanthropy committee who administer grants or loans to community ventures. We should target them."

"Great idea! How do we do that?"

"Well, Clair's taking a Business course at the City College, and we've already discussed a plan for the next phase. I'll contact people I know in companies and set up meetings. Clair will do a presentation, and I'll back her up with the financials. We'll get money from them and use it to win the auction."

Everyone applauded enthusiastically.

Except Clair, whose eyes were round with horror. "I can't do that … I can't stand up and —"

Sid interrupted. "I'm just a number cruncher, I can't do it. Your passion is working with horses, Clair, and helping challenged youngsters. We can work together, but you need to give people your vision, so they'll give us the money."

Clair turned desperately to Steph. "Help me, please! It sounds so simple when Sid says it like that, but you know, I'm terrified of speaking in public. Please tell them–I freeze and can't remember a thing."

Clair's hands clutched at each other in her lap and Steph nodded gloomily. "Yeah, at school the teachers waited and waited for her to start speaking, but then needed to go on to the next person. In the end, we skipped school on show-and-tell days."

Sid frowned. "Oh, dear. I'm sorry, Clair, I didn't know that. If it's impossible for you, then of course, we must think again. But we also need to be realistic. Without that kind of funding, we'll be waving goodbye to Summerfield Stables in January."

Chapter 6

On his way back to the Manor House the driver of the disability van sneaked glances in the rearview mirror. His passenger was hunched in the wheelchair, his eyes closed, and fists clenched.

"Are you okay?"

In reply, David let rip with a mouthful of colorful Army language and the driver burst out laughing. His brother was in the British Army. The words were not directed at him or anyone else, and it was the most impressive performance he'd ever heard! Even better, when he unloaded the wheelchair, David slipped him a large tip.

"Sorry about that."

"It's quite okay, sir. I look forward to driving you again."

* * *

David wheeled himself up the wooden ramp by the front steps just as Cilla came out, dressed for the gym. "Hello! Back so soon? Your riding lesson didn't go well?"

"Yes, I'm back. No, it didn't."

He swung into his sitting room, hoping she'd take the hint and keep on going.

But Cilla followed him and perched on the arm of a couch, swinging her leg. "They shouldn't have sent you there. Clair Williams is useless, and the whole place is a dump. I told you so."

David looked at her, but Cilla was critically examining her designer leggings and aerobics shoes. "I spoke with Anthony earlier. Those London Queensgate apartments are selling for millions. You should sell yours while the market is hot. You can't live alone anymore, so we could move you here permanently."

David wheeled his chair to the door and kicked it viciously with his good leg. It slammed back against the wall. The handle dug a hole and a big chunk of plaster flew across the room. Cilla looked at him, her eyes wide.

"Let's get this straight once and for all, shall we?" David's voice was quiet but dangerous. "I won't be selling my London apartment, under any circumstances. I intend to fully recover and rejoin my Regiment. I'm grateful for everything you've done for me, but this is a temporary arrangement."

He turned the wheelchair towards the bathroom. "And don't discuss my business with anyone, not even Anthony. I have things to do, so go to the gym, or wherever you were going when you decided to interfere in my life again."

* * *

"Ninety-nine … one hundred."

David completed the full set of push-ups, sweat glistening on his muscled back. In the London rehab center, when he was not eating, sleeping, or being examined by doctors, he'd been working to get fit again. Finn, his physical therapist, had sighed. "We can't even measure you for an advanced prosthetic until your wounds are fully healed. I understand the obsession, but you need a fitness plan that supports lower limb surgery."

"You can call it obsession, but I'll go completely crazy if I'm not progressing."

"You are definitely progressing in general fitness, but amputation is a whole different journey. You need to be patient."

David snarled.

* * *

He was stretching, lying on his back, when there was a knock at the door. At his shout to come in, Anthony stuck his head inside and David grinned up at his older brother, "Hey!"

"Hey, you too. Can I come in? I met Cilla heading out and she said you bit her head off."

David rolled into a sitting position. "The Florence Nightingale act was getting to me. Great to see you, Ant. Will you pass me the towel on that chair?"

Anthony allowed no one except David to shorten his name. In spite of the age difference of almost twenty years, the two brothers had built a good relationship. Anthony's mother, Sir George's first wife, had died when he was young and of the three siblings, he looked most like Sir George. He had trained in banking and investment. When George retired, Anthony took over the financial empire and he was heir to the Manor House. Board members and the staff trusted Anthony. He was shorter than David, stocky with twinkly eyes, receding grey hair, and a small, white beard.

He passed the towel to his brother, undid the jacket buttons of his charcoal-colored business suit, and sat down on a couch. David draped the towel around his neck and swung himself into an easy chair opposite him.

"What's up with Cilla, anyway? She's acting very strangely."

"I think she's bored. Maybe looking for a new project?"

David stopped in the middle of pulling a t-shirt over his head and looked alarmed. He continued and grinned at his brother as his head emerged. Anthony roared with laughter as David pulled the t-shirt down over his torso. "I'm relieved to see you almost in one piece. How are you doing?"

David zipped a black jogging top over the t-shirt. "Truthfully?"

"Of course. They were too busy saving your life in the hospital for us to talk, then you were on massive doses of medication. I asked Cilla to get these rooms converted for you and you're looking a lot better. This is your home again, for as long as you want it."

David stared out the window. "I'm lucky to have you and Cilla to help, but I feel trapped. I'm a soldier. I can't wait to get back to the military world where I belong."

"It's going to take time." Anthony's voice was sympathetic, but David's laugh was bitter. "Everyone keeps telling me that. I see danger everywhere; I get panic attacks, then I'm slammed with vertigo. I'm forty. How long before my skills are out of date, and there'll be no going back?"

Anthony leaned forward, rested his elbows on his knees, and looked straight at David. "Knowing you, if there was an easy answer, you'd have found it by now. How about being consciously counter-intuitive? Like, relax and walk in nature, as well as pumping weights? Maybe you're trying to do things so fast that it's slowing you down?"

"Like, trying to run with a prosthetic, before I can walk with it?"

They grinned at each other. "Yeah, something like that."

"Yeah, well, enough of me, what about you, big bro? Rolling in money and well able to retire, yet showing no signs of doing that? It's been a long time since your divorce. Where's the fabulous woman you were going to share the Manor House with? I'm waiting for you to marry someone young and produce an heir."

Anthony sighed. He loosened the patterned silk tie and leaned back among the cushions, interlinking his fingers over a rather portly stomach.

"I get tired of Dad bringing up stuff like that every time I go to visit him. He lives permanently on his yacht now and flirts with all his female caregivers.

Every now and then, the Captain calls and asks me to please fly to Greece or somewhere, meet up, and sort out the mayhem."

David laughed and leaned to press an electric bell. "Where is he now?"

"Cruising around the Mediterranean. It's warm, so I think he'll stay there. As for me and lovely women, I'm an investment banker and not at all sexy. I enjoy evenings at my Club, watching cricket and rugby with friends, and I love wine and good food, probably too much. There are plenty of gold diggers around, but no one real. I feel too old for online dating."

"It's that white beard that puts them off. You better watch out or someone will ask you to play Father Christmas."

They were laughing when Mrs. Jessop knocked. Anthony stood and walked to the mirror to fix his tie and David's shoulders drooped momentarily. "You can't stay for dinner?"

"Sorry, I'm the guest of honor at a company event in Oxford. Maybe next week? I'll give you a call."

Anthony lived in London and, as on previous evenings, David ate dinner alone in front of the big-screen TV. He was watching the European Cup soccer match but muted the sound as Mrs. Jessop brought in his tray.

"Thank you, that looks delicious. Cilla's not around?"

"No, sir. She's often out to dinner with friends."

"Okay, I'll ring when I'm done, and thanks for having the lock fitted on the hall door."

David ate Cornish crab with brown bread and butter, then a delicious beef casserole, with a selection of fresh vegetables. A deep-dish apple pie followed, with thick cream. He did not drink wine because of the medications, but after the hospital food, he thoroughly enjoyed his dinner. David imagined Cilla drinking cocktails with friends they'd both known in the past. But tonight, he could lock his door, so at least she wouldn't be barging in for a midnight chat. The last thing he wanted was a visit from his sister on some bizarre version of night duty.

The soccer ended, David turned off the television, and Mrs. Jessop came for his tray. "Good night, sir, sleep well."

He locked the door and choked back a thickness in his throat. He missed the other guys, the close military living, and even the teasing in rehab. Who could he call? But it was late, and what would he say?

David changed the dressings and swallowed pills. Maybe he should try different tactics, like Anthony had suggested? For some reason, Clair Williams came into his thoughts. Nurses at the amputee center were familiar with injuries like his. He experienced again the allergic reaction at the thought of Clair and two strange females touching him.

But he also remembered the hurt in Clair's eyes and regretted speaking so harshly. Would anyone care if he just accepted vertigo and the wheelchair? He thought perhaps Clair Williams might. Maybe he should he call and apologize? "Pull yourself together, man."

David found his laptop, sat up in bed and did emails. He did not sleep until the early hours of the morning.

Shards of light appeared on his bed from the moon shining through the branches of the magnolia tree. His left leg was tangled in the bed covers and he awoke with a jump. David could distinctly 'feel' the right leg and a panic attack started. He struggled to switch on the lamp and lay panting. He told himself that of course, it wasn't the leg, it was only a body memory.

The barn owls hooted from Potlatch Wood, as they had when he was a boy, and a dog barked faintly from the village. "All you need to do to change your behavior is change your mind."

How often had he said that to trainees! And he

had not died in the bomb blast. Others did, and he resolved to channel his guilt into more realistic goals. He needed to have greater patience. He owed it to them.

* * *

At 10:00 a.m., after breakfast in his room, David changed his schedule. It was a beautiful autumn day. He'd try Anthony's suggestion and take the prosthetic for a walk in the gardens.

He sat on the bed to slide a soft white sock over the stump of his leg and a running shoe onto his left foot. The silicon sleeve of the prosthetic rolled tightly up his right thigh and fastened with straps around his waist. Shirt on, pants on, sweater and jacket on, David put weight on the leg and stood carefully, holding on to the bed. Balancing with his two canes, he took a tentative step and then another.

Vertigo threatened, but he clung to the doorframe and breathed into it. Slowly, he eased out of his room and navigated the hallway, swinging the prosthetic like a pendulum with each step.

Outside, he progressed along the path between the flowerbeds. Then his soldier's eye caught a tiny movement. Cilla was standing well back from an upstairs window, watching him.

With the next swing of the prosthetic, David turned onto the private path to St. Peter's church. Anthony's mother had worshipped there, and from the Manor House, a paved walkway had been laid between the yew trees. Trying to smoothly coordinate his leg and the canes, David swung out of sight of the house, the prosthetic dragging through the leaves like a reluctant puppy. He reached the edge of the churchyard when, bouncing out of a side path, his tail wagging, came a real puppy! Or rather, a young brown-and-white spaniel.

David spotted Ted Williams sitting on the only bench, pouring coffee from a thermos flask into a cup.

"Hi, Ted, sorry to disturb you. I need to rest, could I sit on this bench with you for a few minutes?"

Ted moved his backpack. He had known David a little before he went into the military. "You're welcome, 'though I'd be obliged if you didn't tell anyone that Jossie was with me. Dogs aren't allowed in the churchyard, and quite right too. But I keep him under control. I come here most days to visit my wife and he's company."

David lowered himself onto the seat and sighed with relief as the pressure eased. Ted stroked the dog's ears and beside them, the grave was beautifully laid out with flowering plants. David leaned forward and read the inscription.

"I was sorry to hear of your loss. Mrs. Williams was a lovely lady and I used to buy fruit from her at the farmer's market. You must miss her very much."

"I do." Ted rubbed a hand over a whiskery face. "They say time heals all wounds, but I don't think it does. We just go on living the best we can. But we'll be together again one day." He followed David's eyes. "The other names on there are my son, Ted, Clair's mum … and Owen, our young grandson, all killed in a car crash."

"I remember young Ted, but I didn't know about the accident."

"You've been away a long time." Ted's hand rested absently on the dog's head. "But I expect you've heard about our lease and the auction. I've been a stupid old fool, taking it for granted things were written down. I wish May were here; she handled things so much better than I do." Ted paused in his thoughts and looked at David. "But what about you, young man? You've had a tough time. How are you getting on now?"

Ted's eyes were kind, like his granddaughter's, and David indicated his prosthetic leg. "Frankly, I'm not improving as fast as I should be. I'm working to master the prosthetic, but sometimes get vertigo so badly I can't even stand up. And it's unpredictable."

He massaged his thigh. "I keep reliving the

explosion, haunted by the people who died. I feel guilty for being alive. I try to count my blessings, but I feel angry, so angry all the time"

David was afraid he was losing it and struggled to stand up. Ted did not watch him or attempt to help, for which he was grateful.

"Are you following the soccer?"

"I certainly am. It's the only sport on TV worth watching at the moment. Who do you support?"

"Manchester United, of course."

David smiled. "Yeah, me too. Quarter final on Friday night—that should be an exciting game."

Ted scratched his ear. "Clair doesn't enjoy watching soccer; she'll be studying, or running a jumping class, or something. May used to bring her knitting to sit and cheer with me but it's no fun watching alone. Would you fancy coming over to watch the game?"

"I'd like that. But I don't have any knitting."

Ted's face crinkled. "The knitting's optional; you could bring some beer, instead."

Chapter 7

The next morning, Patricia looked up from her computer as Clair came in. "The Land Agent and other people have arrived for the viewing. Are you ready, or shall I take them into the training room?"

Clair made a face. "I'm as ready as I'll ever be."

She walked through to the yard, glad that Jim, their village taxi driver, had taken Ted to his dental appointment in Oxford.

Quentin was handing out colored flyers to the people gathered there and Clair pasted on a smile. "Good morning, everyone. I think you know that Summerfield Stables is a working yard, and I've asked staff to carry on as usual. Please be aware that children are having lessons. You may not take photographs where they are."

Clair scanned the group. Kyle stood with Gary

Kidd and she quickly broke eye contact. Cilla and her 'horsey set' stood apart from the dairy farmers and other folk. They were dressed in immaculate country outfits.

Cilla strolled over, a strappy purse shaped like a horseshoe swinging from one shoulder. "How exciting to be able to see everything in detail at last. I just can't wait for the auction! This place has such potential."

"It's a work in progress–and I can't believe you want to take it away from disabled children."

She cast her eyes to heaven. "Dear Clair, sentimental as always. There are plenty of other places for them to ride." Cilla was thoroughly enjoying needling Clair in public. "That arena is far more suited to dressage."

Clair ached to strangle her, but Steph appeared at the door to Reception and waved.

"Important phone call in the office."

Forcing her fists to unclench, Clair walked back into the building.

Steph grinned. "There's no phone call, but I could see her smirking and your blood pressure rising. The Bartlett-Browns think they own everything–but they don't own Summerfield Stables."

Yet.

The word hung silently in the air between them.

* * *

When Clair returned, the group had split. Kyle was showing off to Gary as if he owned the place and she followed his finger, pointing out different aspects of the landscape. She ached for this special place that she loved. A blue tractor chugged down a lane in the distance, towing a trailer of root crops. Ridges of chocolate-brown earth stretched beyond that, and a male pheasant called from Potlatch Wood. Gary muttered, "Wish I had my gun."

Quentin opened the gate to May's garden, and Clair winced at his booming voice. "Do come in and feel free to look around Stables Cottage." Gary and Kyle strolled over to join the others.

Clair had put all the personal things away and locked her bedroom door. She got a kick out of Kyle's disappointment when he tried to open it. The cottage was spotless, although Clair knew the kitchen needed remodeling. But all May's copper pans were polished until they shone, and Clair loved her hand-embroidered cushions. Cilla's friends were laughing between themselves saying everything in the cottage should go to a charity shop.

Unable to listen anymore, Clair went outside and sat on a bench. But the windows were open and

Gary Kidd's voice floated out. "I'll rip it all out and make it super modern, like black and white, with an open floor plan. That garden will be the first thing to go. I'll concrete it over. My cars can't be parked in the same place as delivery trucks."

At last, Quentin shepherded them out, fussing and clucking. "Clair will now take you around the stable block, and I'll end by reminding you of the auction on January 3rd. I look forward to seeing you again then."

Cool and professional, Clair led the group into the pony barn. "These original stables were built by the Duke for his carriage horses and hunters. We added the indoor arena in—"

She was interrupted by an outraged shout. Steph held Gary's cell phone up in the air, then casually flipped it into a nearby bucket of water. "You heard, Gary Kidd. You don't photograph my son, nor any of our children."

At last, it was over, and Ted arrived home.

"How was the dentist?"

"Fine."

He asked nothing about the viewing, took the plated meal Clair had kept warm for him, and went into his room with Jossie. She heard the TV go on and stared at his closed door. Lots of landlords didn't allow pets; if they lost the lease, they'd need to find somewhere to rent where they could keep a dog. It would be tight, financially but, thank goodness, Ted still had his pension money, to tide them over till she found another job.

* * *

It was her afternoon and evening at the college! Robert was on duty, so Clair changed her clothes and put on light makeup. It had been windy, with heavy clouds all day and it started to rain heavily as she drove to Oxford.

The windshield wipers on the Jeep swished from side to side in time with her thoughts. Sid had persuaded her to try presentations at two companies that he knew well, and anxiety gnawed at her. "They won't judge us harshly, and their sponsorship would boost the auction fund big time."

Clair shivered. But her Business Plan was almost ready, and today they would meet the experienced mentors assigned to help them. She hoped desperately that her mentor knew about presentations.

Driving carefully along the narrow lanes in the rain, Clair was almost late. It was early afternoon, but there were lights on in all the classrooms and they reflected in the puddles. There were no spaces near to the building and Clair held her belted fawn raincoat tightly around her as the rainy gusts blew her across the parking lot. She walked carefully, trying to avoid splashes on her new jeans.

The class was made up of twenty mature, working students like herself, squeezing time from small businesses to learn management skills. Settled into her seat by the window, Clair shook the raindrops from her hair and smiled. She saw admiration on the faces of guys watching her and decided to forget her worries and enjoy today. She normally went straight home after evening class, but last week, a couple of guys had suggested she go for coffee with them. Clair hadn't had a date in a long time, so she bought a pretty sweater online, found earrings that matched, then added a brighter lipstick than she normally wore.

The course tutor entered. "Good afternoon. Great to see you all, and we'll be completing the Business Planning module now. I'll be introducing your mentors in the last session."

When the bell rang after the break, they returned to their seats. The Head of Faculty entered with the course tutor and a small group of people.

Clair's eyes widened. One of them was David Bartlett-Brown, out of his wheelchair and walking with two canes. Their eyes briefly connected before she looked down at her laptop.

Please, oh please, don't let him be my mentor!

* * *

David had spotted Clair immediately. She was seated between two young guys, looking attractive in a red sweater, slim, fitted jeans, and suede ankle boots. One leg was crossed confidently over the other, but when she saw him, she uncrossed her legs and looked down. The visitors were asked to introduce themselves and David gripped the corner of the desk to anchor himself. He had chosen a navy blazer, pressed chinos, and a crisp, white shirt for the occasion and trimmed his beard. Both feet were clad in expensive leather shoes. He smiled around the room.

"Good evening. I'm David Brown, a Captain in the British Army, currently on Leave because of injury. I have a first degree in Planning, a Masters in Management, and served on tours of duty in Iraq and Afghanistan. My last was as Senior Instructor at the Afghani National Training College."

* * *

Clair registered little of the other introductions. Her heart was beating way too fast and she needed to run away from this dangerous man. She packed her things surreptitiously, and at the closing bell for the session, sprinted for the college office. On the notice board outside was the list of the students and their mentors.

The administrator was shutting down her system and looked pointedly at the clock as Clair dived through the door. "Please excuse me, but this is really important. I've been assigned David Brown as my mentor on the Management module. Is there any chance of changing?"

The administrator stood up and began to throw things into her bag impatiently. "I don't think you understand, Miss Williams. This course is in the evening and it's almost impossible to find anyone willing to be a mentor. You live in the same village as Mr. Brown, and he has mobility problems."

Clair waited for her to say, 'Duh,' like Nick did, but she was not of that generation. "I know it's logical, but there are other issues. It simply won't work."

The administrator's eyes flicked over her shoulder and Clair knew David had entered the office behind her. "Well, thank you, anyway. Good night."

She marched across the office and out of the door

leading directly onto the parking lot. Everyone else had gone. The only vehicle still sitting in the dark and rain was the Stables Jeep. So much for dressing up to go for coffee after class!

Clair pulled on her raincoat and walked doggedly across the parking lot, no longer caring about splashes on new jeans. Opening the driver's door, a fierce gust of wind snatched it away and slammed it shut again. Muttering curses, Clair wrenched it open once more and struggled to climb in. She turned the ignition key. The engine responded with horrible grinding noises that went on and on.

"Come on, it's only a little rain! We aren't beaten by this, are we?"

Clair often talked to the Jeep as if it were a horse; and it sometimes worked. She hopped out again, into the downpour and opened the hood. Even after trying all her usual, sure-fire methods, the engine did not start.

From the corner of her eye, she saw David Brown with his canes, walking slowly along a covered walkway to the Disabled Parking area. "Brilliant, that's all I need!"

She stuck her head back under the hood and prayed he'd drive past. But no such luck–his car approached and stopped.

"Can I give you a ride home?"

David's voice was the last thing Clair wanted to hear, but a huge puddle was now lapping at her best boots. She came out from under the hood and looked at him, biting her lower lip.

"I can drop you back at the Stables, and you could have it towed tomorrow."

Clair wanted to stick her nose in the air and say she was just fine and dandy. But the rain was now literally bouncing off her and the Jeep. Then it turned to huge hailstones and she began to laugh.

"I accept! Or I might be the first student to drown in a college parking lot!"

Grabbing her bag, Clair locked the Jeep and ran around to the passenger side of David's car. She clambered into the warm, dry interior.

"Whew! It's wild out there."

* * *

Clair's hair was plastered flat to her head. She dripped as she fastened her seatbelt and David smiled in the darkness. The rain had given him a second chance. He switched on the heater and drove slowly across the flooded parking lot.

"Is this a Jaguar? It's much lower than a 4 x4–how do you get into it?"

"Yes, it's a vintage Jag Dad gave me on my

eighteenth birthday. It's been in storage since I went into the Army, but it's fun to drive and a bit of a test for me." He turned onto the Summerfield road. "The prosthetic was difficult at first, but I remembered those monkeys with the stripy tails—I've forgotten what they're called …"

"Lemurs?"

"Yes, lemurs. I've seen them on TV. They swing with their arms and use their tail for leverage. I hold onto the roof, position my left leg inside and then swing the prosthetic in, like a lemur. Whatever works, right?"

"Right."

They continued in silence but when they stopped at a traffic light, David turned his head and Clair saw his face in the red glow.

"I heard what you said in the office and I want to apologize for my behavior at the Stables. Students usually request me as a mentor, not ask for a transfer."

The light changed and he drove on. "It's no excuse, but I was in a lot of pain that day. I should have cancelled the assessment, but I was afraid I'd lose my nerve and not do it at all."

Clair relaxed. Jack was right, his rude manner had been from pain and the awkwardness of the situation.

"Apology accepted. I told Jack Harris I had no experience with veterans, but he said you couldn't travel to our London facility. I need to apologize too. I was nervous, and we needed to talk for much longer before doing a physical assessment."

Then the conversation flowed easily as they drove back to Summerfield. Heavy rain continued to pound on the roof.

"Could we start again, Clair?" David said as he pulled up beside Stables Cottage. "I need riding lessons to help overcome vertigo; you're looking for support with business presentations. We both have deadlines, could we help each other?"

Chapter 8

Clair was on early stable duty next morning and Ted was up when she left the cottage. He didn't ask her to feed the chickens, and when she came back for her lunchtime break, the table was set for two. Ted had made omelets.

"I found the ham in the fridge, collected the eggs, and picked some spinach."

He sat next to her while they ate and looked pleased when Clair laid her fork across her empty plate with a sigh. "Delicious!"

"I'm sorry the lease thing hit me so hard, dear. I'll pull my weight better from now on."

Clair realized it was natural for their roles to reverse as he grew older, and she needed to look after him now. But Ted's eyes were alive again.

Whatever had caused that change, Clair was glad of it.

She jumped up and gave him a hug. "We've gone through bad times before. Like you always say, it'll be okay in the end."

Ted got up to load the dishwasher. "I know that things were a bit awkward for you with David Bartlett-Brown the other day. But I met him when I was sitting with May and I think he's lonely. I hope you don't mind, but I've invited him to watch the soccer game with me tonight."

Clair laughed as she passed him plates and silverware. "How strange is that? I was about to mention that David and I met again at the college yesterday. He apologized for his meltdown and wants to come back for lessons. He's also my college mentor. He's coming over before the game, to help with my business presentation."

* * *

The Staff meeting began with Robert reporting on the Sponsored Ride. "The course is mapped and we're matching riders with mounts. Lots of people in the village are signing up to support our youngsters."

He pinned a big chart on the board.

Steph laughed and wrinkled her nose. "Yeah, lots of commuters are beginning to worry about a chicken farm in Summerfield. Thousands of chickens smell a lot worse than a few horses. It looks like delivery trucks would be coming and going all hours of the day and night."

"How are the bake sales going?"

Patricia shook a box of money and passed it to Sid. "Parents are enthusiastic about making baked goods, and our students are more than enthusiastic about eating them!"

Sid opened the box packed with paper money and coins. "Cake is happening! How about the bank presentation? Not long till our first company visit."

Everyone looked at Clair and she shifted uncomfortably in her seat. "I get goosebumps thinking about it, but I'll be ready. I now have a college mentor to help me."

For some reason, she didn't tell them the name of her mentor. No one would have believed her if she had!

* * *

At five o'clock, Clair dashed to the cottage to shower and change. It felt as if the shower bubbles were caught beneath her ribs when she ran downstairs to answer the door.

"Hi, come on in. Granddad's taken Jossie for a quick walk before the kick-off. Would you like coffee?"

"Thanks, black, no sugar."

David was out of his wheelchair and walking with his canes again. He hung up his coat and joined Clair at the kitchen table, where her laptop and college files lay open.

"The Business Plan you sent me was excellent and you clearly understand not-for-profit organizations"

She put mugs of coffee in front of them and sat down.

"For your presentation, start by imagining I'm a potential investor. Give me some reasons why our company should give you money for 'Riding with Challenges.'"

Clair's hands shook and she took deep breaths. "This is difficult for me. Um … when someone comes to us, we study the recommendations from doctors and physical therapists. Each client has an assessment, then …"

"Sorry, it's too boring."

She put her elbow on the table between them, to shield herself from his harsh opinions. David saw this.

More gently, he said, "Try and sell me on what people get when they come here. What is it you want me to sponsor?"

Clair thought, eyes cast upward for inspiration.

"Okay ... our challenged students have disabilities and riding builds their core strength. We've purchased, commissioned, and invented special equipment for them and trained our ponies to help. People who are damaged physically are afraid and hurt inside. Horses are prey animals and understand fear. Treated kindly, they want to be with humans for security, like being in a herd. When we help a student with challenges connect with a horse, it builds trust and confidence in them both."

* * *

David tried to listen actively, and not be distracted by Clair's beautiful, kissable mouth. He leaned back, his arms behind his head, and watched her face as she spoke.

When she finished, he came back from where his thoughts had taken him. "That's good, but it needs more personal passion. You're asking us for a lot of money, to give these young people a better future. Why do you care so much about this?"

Clair looked down at her clasped hands and back

at him. She started to speak, stopped, then began again.

"My brother, Owen, was born with Down syndrome. People stared at his almond-shaped eyes and a tongue that stuck out. To us, he was a cheeky, laughing boy, and his challenges made no difference to our love for him. But Granddad taught me to ride. Owen loved the ponies too, but there was no expertise or equipment available for him. He cried because he was excluded, and I cried with him."

Thinking about Owen, Clair forgot her fear. "Children come to us with bodies that don't work well; but they are accepted, unconditionally. Their pony becomes a special friend. We aim to support their development and applaud their achievements. With his parents' permission, I've put together some video clips of Zach."

She cued her laptop. "He was ten when he first came to us. I've been documenting his progress for a year."

David focused on the screen.

"Here he is, when he first started riding. He's barely able to sit up in the saddle and is silent. Through twice-weekly lessons, Zach's muscles have strengthened, he needs less medication and he's begun to laugh and chat. Here's the video I made of him last week."

On the screen, a volunteer led a small brown pony toward the camera, ridden by the same boy. He was smiling. Another volunteer walked beside him. "Can you turn Bonnie this way, Zach? Well done. Can you stretch up and grab that balloon?"

Clair paused on a close-up of Zach's face as he reached for an orange balloon and he looked like a different boy. She smiled. "As well as building muscle, we try to strengthen self-esteem. Our volunteers are coached to observe and listen. Zach is out of his wheelchair, high on a pony, and having fun. He's just one child–we work with lots of others. If Summerfield Stables loses the lease, the support we give to youngsters like Zach will end. We're asking for your investment, to continue this vital work."

The door latch clicked and Jossie bounded in. "Oh, you, soggy doggy!" Clair jumped up and grabbed a dog towel. She was wiping his dirty paws when Ted came in and shut the door behind him.

"Hello, David; cold night out there."

"Evening, Ted; yes, I reckon there'll be a frost tonight."

Ted divested himself of gloves, overcoat, scarf, and hat. "It's a potlatch night, for sure. In the old days, we'd wake up at midnight when they rang the church bells. I'd go out with my dad and we'd uncover our potlatch boulders. In the morning, hey presto, Roofing tiles! Like the slices of a nice, round, cottage loaf."

He sat on the old chair by the door to take off his boots and slip his feet into comfy, old tweed slippers. "I've walked the dog and shut the chickens in for the night. Now I'm going to relax and watch soccer."

He walked through to his room and switched on the TV. A dry Jossie bounded after him and he called back to them.

"Are you done with your college work? The teams are warming up."

Clair looked inquiringly at David and he stood up, pivoting on his sound leg. "I think we've finished for tonight. That last part was convincing, Clair, and I felt motivated to help. You could spend a few minutes jotting down what you said, to read through before your presentation. Ted, the beer's by the front door. I struggled to carry it with my canes."

Ted came back and picked up the box. "Um… non-alcoholic?"

"Those on the top are for me, because I'm still on a lot of meds. The real stuff is underneath. I just need to check with Clair. Are we still on for tomorrow's lesson?"

Clair called over her shoulder as she took Jossie's wet towel to the utility room. "All set. Robert's available and suggested we use Winston. Jack Harris is coming to help you mount and dismount, until your muscles are stronger."

Clair washed her hands and slipped three pizzas into the oven. She wrote notes as David had suggested, until the aroma of toasted cheese and Italian herbs filled the kitchen.

* * *

Ted's eyes were glued to the screen when Clair placed the tray with pizzas for him and David on the low coffee table.

"Thanks, those smell good."

David was aware of her closeness, then she went back into the kitchen and closed the door behind her.

On the bookcase behind Ted there was a big framed photo. In it, a smiling man, 'Young Ted,' held the hand of a little girl. His arm was around a lovely woman holding a baby in her arms. He and Ted ate pizza and watched the flow of play. Half-time break came with advertisements and a recruitment clip for the British Army.

Ted muted the sound. "You don't need to tell me,

but what were you doing in Afghanistan? I thought all our troops were home now."

David tilted his can and took a sip. "You're right, the main British and American forces were pulled out. But the biggest drug smuggling rings in the world still operate from there to fund international terrorism. We have a commitment to support the National government, and I helped to train Afghani officers."

"Sounds important, but dangerous?"

"Yes, but that's what the Army does and it's my life. When I get this vertigo under control, there'll be another role for me somewhere."

"Here we go again." Ted clicked the sound back on. "Let's hope for more action this half. We'd be a goal ahead, if it wasn't for that penalty."

They were soon back with the crowd and cheered as their team won and went through to the next round. "Can you come over and watch the semi-final?"

"I'd like that. It's much more fun to watch with another supporter. If you and Clair like Italian food, would you like me to make dinner? I enjoy cooking and the herbs in your garden would make a great pasta sauce."

Ted grinned, and picked up the tray, "You're on! It'll be a nice change from pizza."

David's left leg was numb. He stretched it slowly before he followed Ted to the kitchen. He was gazing at Clair, who had fallen asleep at the table. Her head was pillowed on her files, and soft tendrils of hair curled on her cheek. Her face was the little girl in the photo.

She did not stir when Ted gently closed her laptop. "I'll see you out before I wake her, or she'll be embarrassed." Ted sounded lost and concerned. "She's such a good girl, and we're in a terrible mess because of this lease."

David wasn't listening. It was physically impossible, of course, but he had an insane urge to take Clair in his arms, rest her head on his shoulder, and carry her to bed.

Chapter 9

David was serving himself breakfast from the buffet that Mrs. Jessop had laid in the dining room.

"When are you going to shave off that scruffy beard?"

He turned his head to grin at his sister. "I've been clean-shaven all my adult life. I'll shave before I go back to military duty; meanwhile, I shall grow it longer and longer, just to annoy you."

Cilla pulled a face and joined him at the dining table with her breakfast. "I'm glad to see you a bit more cheerful, anyway. Why not come out with us on Friday? There's a Quiz Night at the pub and lots of my girlfriends want to see you again."

David buttered a slice of toast. "Thanks, but I start riding lessons today, to help the vertigo. It's too soon."

Cilla poured coffee. "Later, then. You know Zara's divorced and she has several horses. She'd be delighted to help you."

Mrs. Jessop came in. "Major Harris is here, sir."

"Great! See you later, Cilla."

David swung his wheelchair away from the table. His leg would be under strain today, so he'd decided not to walk. He smiled cheerfully as Jack loaded him into the van. "Thanks for coming today; it'll make things a lot easier and you can see the setup."

"You're welcome." Jack touched a crimson rose that still bloomed by the driveway and inhaled the scent. "Look at that! Tucked away out of the wind."

They drove through the village and this time David ignored people staring at the van. It was what it was. He was in a wheelchair but moving forward with his plans.

"I'm glad you worked things out with Clair. She's learning more about amputee trauma and asked for campaign videos from Afghanistan. She's going to be documenting your progress from today, to see if riding improves vertigo. I can use that for your assessment, but only if you accept that it's a learning curve and go easy on her."

David glanced over his shoulder, interested in the warmth of Jack's voice. "You like her, don't you?"

Jack grinned. "Of course. She cares a lot about her students."

"And she's pretty?"

"Yeah, that too."

Robert came out of the building to meet them. "Hi. I've made sure no one else is around for your lesson today."

He was leading the way through the horse barn when David suddenly jerked the wheelchair to a halt. His eyes were riveted on four sacks, newly delivered and waiting to go into the store. He gasped. "Fertilizer!"

Jack squatted next to him and Robert came in on the other side. David's head was down, his voice robotic and far away.

"Insurgents pack batteries and fuses into fertilizer. Pressure closes the circuit. It blows."

Robert quickly pulled open the top of a sack and held a handful of pony nuggets near David's nose. "It's pony feed, not fertilizer."

David half-opened his eyes and looked at the nuts in Robert's cupped hands. He was panting and shaky but regaining control.

Jack put a hand on his arm. "Hang in there, you're okay."

"May I push you to meet Winston?"

David nodded and Robert took hold of the

handles. "He's a special horse and knows about explosions too."

The radio was playing quietly from the tack room as Robert took David to the loading ramp. There were three riding helmets to try, and one fit him perfectly. David waited, out of his wheelchair and leaning on Jack, then Robert led Winston across the smooth sand. He was a big solid horse with a handsome face like a charger for a knight of old. He stood quietly, looking at them with dark, liquid eyes that seemed to ask, "So, what have we here?"

Robert lifted the saddle flap, smoothed Winston's coat, and cinched the girth a little tighter. "We don't want this pinching, do we, old fella? David, Jack and I are going to help you mount, and will be with you for this lesson. I told Clair I'd call her when we're ready."

He nudged Winston closer to the ramp and gave David his arm. He and Jack supported him to put his left foot in the stirrup. David hauled the prosthetic leg up and over Winston's back. It wasn't elegant, but the big horse stood like a rock. Inside the prosthetic sleeve, David's leg began to throb.

Robert looked up at him. "I have a back injury and Winston has only partial sight in one eye. He's my horse now, but I trained him when he belonged to the Mounted Police. We were controlling crowds at a football game when someone started throwing firecrackers. A drunken hooligan punched Winston in the eye. He reared, and I was pulled off." Robert paused, "After that, neither of us returned to duty. But you're going to be fine, and everyone is here to help you."

* * *

Clair watched David through the small observation port in the office, noticing when he tensed with pain. She walked out into the arena.

"Hi, David, good morning, Jack. Let's start with a slow walk and some gentle, stretching exercises."

Robert led Winston and Jack walked on the side away from Clair.

"Try to relax into the saddle and think of rolling your body gently to the rhythm of Winston's walk. Good, now, look to your right as you pass the wall mirrors. Can you correct that slight lean? Jack, would you help with that?"

After a few minutes, she saw him go pale. "Halt. May I touch your ankle, David?"

He nodded mutely, leaning forward with his eyes closed. Clair adjusted the stirrup on his undamaged side, watching his face regain some color and chatting quietly about different muscle groups. David opened his eyes again.

"Well done. Now, I want you to slowly, slowly, stretch up out of the saddle ... and look forward, between Winston's ears. That's it! Walk on again, please."

A few minutes more and Clair called a halt. "Good work. Fifteen minutes a day is enough to start with. Please call to cancel tomorrow if you are very sore. We can schedule your lesson every second day."

* * *

But every day for the next week, David was there on time.

Soon he could mount with just Robert to help and bit back a protest when his side-walkers became Steph and Victoria. He didn't tell anyone that the stump of his leg rubbed raw in every lesson but hurried back to the Manor House to soak in the tub. He took painkillers, smothered the wound with antiseptic cream, and rested. His attacks of vertigo seemed less frequent.

Was it too early to think he was winning?

After his lesson on Friday, Robert asked him, "Might you be free on Saturday afternoon? I'm running a fundraiser with our able-bodied students, but we're short-staffed. Any chance you could be the announcer for show jumping?"

David liked Robert. "Happy to help; what do I do?"

"You sit on the stage at the announcer's table with the microphone. I give you a list and you read out the names of each student as they come in to jump. Clair is scoring."

* * *

David recognized some of the horses and ponies as they came into the arena. They normally worked with challenged students, but today seemed to enjoy the variety and greater freedom.

"Next into the ring is number 24, Madeline Jones, riding Bella. Let's see how she does on this tight course."

In between announcing, David found himself watching Clair. Sand flew beneath Bella's hooves as she skimmed the jumps, the young rider crouched over her neck.

"Well done, Maddie and Bella! An admirable, clear round, and they're through to the jump-off."

At the end of the afternoon, David read out the winners and Clair presented rosettes. There was a Lap of Honor by the riders, with enthusiastic applause from families and friends, and Clair walked over to the announcer's table.

"Thank you so much. You made it sound like the Windsor Horse Show and the students loved it!"

She stood below him on the floor of the arena. He looked down into warm, brown eyes, fringed with dark lashes and discovered she had freckles on her nose. In fawn riding pants, white shirt open at the neck, and tall, black boots, she looked almost edible.

He cleared his throat. "It was fun. I'll do the next one too, if you like."

* * *

Clair was pleased with David's progress, but also with her own on the business presentation. She was becoming more confident each time she practiced it with David. In public, they were instructor and student, rarely speaking except in lessons. Only Ted knew that David was Clair's college mentor, and she hugged that secret close to her heart.

They'd worked for two sessions after college and there was one more before the first bank trip. "Shall we work in the pub tonight, instead of with the janitor cleaning all around us like last week?"

Clair hesitated, "Yes, but could we stop somewhere

closer to Summerfield? Tomorrow is hectic, I have a full day of rehearsals for the Christmas Nativity Ride."

They drove separately to The River Inn in Woodstock and the parking lot was crowded. Clair found a space halfway to the pub and looked at herself in the mirror on the sun visor. She smoothed on soft, red lip gloss. "Enjoy tonight! This is the last time you'll transform into 'Gorgeous Clair, meeting Captain Brown after class.'"

David was waiting by the back door of the pub and she watched him as she walked. He stood tall, in olive-colored jeans, dark green sweater, and tan leather jacket. He'd gained in strength and confidence since he'd started lessons, and now only needed one cane.

He spotted her, and Clair's cheeks flushed. For a split second, their eyes locked, then he laughed and indicated the Jaguar, parked in a Disabled space. "I think that's the only benefit of losing a leg."

The River Inn was an ancient pub with deep, leather armchairs by a blazing log fire. They drank sparkling apple juice, and after a brief look at her presentation, David shut the laptop and passed it back to Clair.

"This is good; I think you're done."

Clair relaxed and stared into the fire. "I love this

pub. In summer or winter, it's so comfortable. I didn't know if you would like it too."

David was gazing at her. "After some of the places I've been posted, I appreciate all things good and beautiful."

There were so many interesting things to share and laugh about, but suddenly, it was closing time. They came out to the parking lot with the sound of wooden balls bouncing down a bowling lane on the far side of the wall.

Clair smiled as people cheered. "Lizzie and I used to come here with the Youth Club. It's a traditional bowling alley, the forerunner of electronic lanes. You bowl with wooden balls, to knock down wooden pins."

David paused at the bottom of the steps, "I hate to ask you, but it's slippery here, and I'd like to walk you to your car. May I hold your arm?"

Clair immediately offered it. Did he really need to hold her arm? Or was it an excuse to draw her close? Whatever, it was nice.

Until a moment later, when Kyle came through an archway from the bowling alley.

"Well, well! Who'd think Miss Snooty Williams would line up with the other girls to kiss our so-called hero?"

Clair burned him with her eyes, and he looked

back with an unpleasant sneer.

"I'm surprised a Bartlett-Brown even bothers to talk to you. Hero? Being blown up is what you expect when you join the military, isn't it?"

David spoke quietly, "That's enough."

Kyle hooted with laughter. "Or what? You'll give me a thrashing? You and whose army?"

He pushed past, deliberately bumping into them.

David moved so fast she didn't see exactly what happened. He seemed to put a hand on the wall, pivot from the waist, and swing his elbow. Kyle landed flat on his back, blood pouring from his nose. He put a hand up to his face and stared at the thick red liquid on his fingers.

"What the …?"

He started to get up, ready to fight, but David was entirely focused and gathered like a coiled spring. Kyle looked uncertain. David was a trained soldier. Even with one leg, he could obviously take care of himself.

"Okay, okay, it was just a joke." Kyle held up his hands in surrender.

Clair picked up the cane and David offered her his arm. "May I escort you to your vehicle, Miss Williams?"

Chapter 10

Clair lay in bed, with her mind racing. Was she falling in love? It was exhilarating to have David around and she wanted to be with him much more.

But the next day she was brought back to earth with a crash.

"I'm sorry to tell you, but my volunteers are all complaining about David." Steph sat down heavily in Patricia's chair. "You get on with him really well, and so does Robert. But the rest of us feel like we are supposed to be Army subordinates: just 'shut up and jump to it.'"

Eyes wide, Clair turned to watch David getting into his wheelchair and chatting with Robert as Victoria led Winston back to his stall. "I must admit, I haven't seen him like that."

"You wouldn't. He thanks you and Robert but

ignores the rest of us. He's just like Cilla, a typical Bartlett-Brown. He comes, he rides, he goes again. He doesn't even bring Winston a treat. We were sympathetic at first, but he's totally on his own agenda."

Steph rubbed a weary hand across her eyes. "When you were rehearsing earlier, Nick had a meltdown. You know what he's like when he loses it. I was really upset, but David looked at me as if I should control my son. You need to give him feedback, or the volunteers say they won't do anything for him anymore."

Clair sat down opposite her. "I didn't even know a storm was brewing. What's going on with Nick?"

"Adolescence, and he's angry because Mum and I are cutting back on some of the foods he loves to eat. He's putting on too much weight. What happens if he gets too heavy to ride Teddy? He's the only pony suitable for Nick to ride; and he's loved him forever."

Steph put her elbows on the desk, face resting in her hands and her eyes shut. "Last night, he stayed in his wheelchair till 1:00 a.m., refusing to go to bed. It's not good for him, and it made me late again this morning. I'm so tired, and this hassle with David Brown is the last straw."

Clair touched her shoulder gently, "I'll make you a coffee."

As the coffee percolated, she thought about Steph. Her husband left; and after a string of low-paid jobs, Steph came to the Stables. Clair could not pay big money, but she could offer flexibility and riding lessons for Nick. Luckily, Steph's mum could help as well, and Clair was delighted to have Steph's energy and good humor at the Stables. But it was tough for a single parent to make ends meet.

Clair put the coffee mug down next to her.

"Thanks." Steph sat up and wrapped her fingers around it. She took several sips and sighed. "Nick's body is changing. He needs a male caregiver, but there's no way we can afford that. Mum and I could manage if we had a mobile hoist. We're saving, but they're expensive."

"I'm sorry, I've been focused on this presentation and didn't know things were so bad. I'll talk to David." Clair looked out again and he was wheeling toward Reception. "I'll catch him now."

She had almost caught up when he went through the outer doors. She stopped short when she heard a joyous shout.

"Kate!"

Through the window in the top of the door she saw a woman in Army fatigues, walking across the parking lot. She looked about the same age as Clair, with a tanned face, and a glorious mane of long, brown hair. Her face was alight with joy as she bent to kiss David on the lips.

"I met your sister at the house. She said you were here, and I couldn't wait; was it okay to come over?"

"Of course! It's great to see you."

David turned at the sound of the door. "Clair, come and meet a colleague from my team. Lieutenant Kate McIntyre, this is Clair Williams, my riding instructor."

They shook hands and Kate looked around the yard. "Your sister didn't seem too impressed, but this place looks great to me."

Clair bit her lip. "Thanks. We try."

Kate turned back to David. "Are you free to take Hannibal for a walk?"

"Hannibal? Wasn't that your dog from Afghanistan?"

She nodded and led them to the Army Jeep. The rear seats had been taken out and a wire crate filled the whole back space. Inside it, a huge dog watched Kate intently, and she touched him through the mesh. He licked her fingers and Kate's voice was husky as she spoke.

"He's a black German Shepherd, crossed with a Rottweiler. Not your normal search-and-rescue dog, and certainly not the best-looking puppy we ever had. But he's super intelligent, with an extraordinary ability to scent."

Hannibal's eyes were his only beauty. One ear was crumpled and ridged with red scars. He looked as if he had mange, but black hair had grown out white wherever he had shrapnel damage. Kate opened the cage door and ruffled the fur on his neck.

"He was one of our best dogs, but since the explosion, he's terrified of loud noises. He throws himself to the ground, burying his head in his paws, and cries when he's left alone."

She caught Clair's expression of sympathy. "Our dogs are Ministry of Defense property. When Hann couldn't work, he was sent back to the UK, as surplus to requirements."

Kate gave him a treat from her pocket. "He's too big and ugly to be adopted. He's passed his end-of-service date, and only has a short time to live."

She looked at them with passionate appeal. "But he's a veteran too, and saved lives. If Hannibal hadn't warned us, David and I would be dead."

David's face was troubled. "I'd take him, but I struggle to manage a prosthetic leg. I don't know what's going to happen in the future, but I'll do everything I can to help find him a home."

Clair offered the back of her hand for Hannibal to

sniff and shook her head regretfully. "I'd love to say yes, but we have a male spaniel who does not like other males. We also run a busy Stables operation and couldn't give him the care he needs."

She didn't add that they might not even be there. "But you can take him for a walk here. Jossie is indoors with my grandfather and there are no ponies in the fields. This top track is a twenty-minute circular route around Potlatch Wood."

Kate clipped a lead onto the harness. Hannibal jumped down from the Jeep. Standing beside her, damaged as he was, he was a magnificent dog with great dignity.

"Good luck in finding him a new home. See you tomorrow, David?"

"Absolutely."

As Clair walked back to the door, she heard David invite Kate to the Manor House. "I'm sore after the lesson. I can't walk with you, but can you stay for lunch? Jack Harris will be here soon to pick me up and my sister could still be at home. She might know someone who could take Hannibal."

"Great! We'll follow you soon, come on, Hann."

A white van turned into the top of the lane as Clair watched Kate and Hannibal jog into the woods. She looked at David at the exact moment he looked at her.

* * *

Steph was grooming Rebel as Clair leaned gloomily on the half-door. Jealousy tugged like indigestion as she recalled Kate kissing David.

"A visitor arrived for David and I had no chance to speak with him about the volunteers. Can you let them know I'll do it tomorrow right after his lesson?"

Steph ran the scraper over the brush and pulled out black hair. "Okay, but right now, you need to go and look in the bottom field."

"Oh no, what else have I've missed?"

"Someone swung by to say that Gary Kidd has purchased two fields from the Duke's Estate. One of them is on the far side of Potlatch Wood, opening onto the Woodstock Road. Apparently, heavy trucks have been seen going down there."

"And the other?"

"The soggy meadow below our fields."

"What is he up to now? I'll get the Jeep and look before afternoon classes begin."

Clair's empty stomach was rumbling and there was no time for lunch. She dived into the office to get the keys for the Jeep and took a muffin from the big box she'd bought from Patricia. They were supposed to be for Ted's afternoon snacks, but on impulse, she took the whole box with her.

Clair parked the Jeep past St. Peter's and walked. Near to where she'd first met Gary Kidd that day, she heard the cough and roar of big diesel engines. All the ponies were working, and the fields were empty. She crossed quietly through Potlatch Wood.

A wide, flexi-metal track had been laid from the gate at the top down to the bottom of the field. Traveling slowly down was an enormous yellow digger, followed by two empty trucks; and several long trailers were parked, loaded with plastic pipes. Clair counted six men in hard hats and orange high-visibility vests.

"Hi, could I speak with the supervisor here?"

The man pointed and when Clair reached him, she opened the box and smiled. "I've brought you some homemade muffins."

The surprised supervisor smiled back, obviously expecting a complaint about noise or something. He signaled, and the engines shut down.

"Break time."

Clair offered the muffins around. "I'm Clair, by the way, from the Stables."

The supervisor looked awkward as he took the last muffin. "Yeah, he said you'd be nosing around."

"I presume 'he' is Gary Kidd?"

"I didn't say that, did I?" He bit into the muffin.

"No. You're just doing your job–and we haven't had this conversation. I can see the track laid to the wet area bordering our fields and guess the diggers are to lay drains. Could you nod, if I'm correct?"

The foreman chewed appreciatively, then he nodded.

"Last question and I'll leave you to it. What for?"

Chapter 11

As they drove back to the Manor House, David told Jack about Kate and Hannibal. He checked in with Mrs. Jessop about lunch and took two strong painkillers. Showered and changed, he heard Kate arrive and Jack chatting with her as they walked Hannibal to the backyard.

In the dining room, Mrs. Jessop had laid cold cuts of beef and chicken, baked jacket potatoes, and salads. Kate smiled up at Jack as he held her chair. David offered her a basket of warm bread rolls. "In case you're wondering, this is my dad's house, not mine."

"Now I see where the posh accent comes from."

"Where's Hannibal?"

"He's tied on a long rope near the kitchen where he can see your housekeeper. She found him a big bone. 'The prisoner ate a last hearty meal' … and all that."

There was a silence. Then they spoke of other things.

* * *

Jack headed off as they moved into the sitting room for coffee. "I can't stay. Nice to meet you, Kate."

David looked at photos on Kate's phone with her and they spoke about the team in Afghanistan. There was a swirl of tires on gravel.

"It's my brother, Anthony. Can you stay a while longer?"

She shook her head. "I need to get back to the base."

Anthony came in, and after introductions, Kate went to get Hannibal. David quickly related his story. The big dog walked to heel without a leash and Kate did a quick obedience display. She looked tearful and it was obvious how much she loved him as she slipped the leash back over his head.

"May I take him for a few minutes?" The big dog looked up at him as Anthony took the leash.

They set off together around the rose beds, and Hannibal was listening to him talking as they walked.

Kate watched them intently. "That's interesting, the guy who trained Hannibal looked a bit like your brother. He was killed in Helmand province; then Hannibal came to me. Might your brother take him?"

David shook his head. "No chance. Anthony's a banker and lives in central London. He's probably sorry for Hannibal, like the rest of us."

Suddenly, an idea struck him. "But there's one last place we could try. You met Cilla–she's got loads of wealthy friends with land and animals. Come to the pub with us before you head back, and I'll call her to meet us there. It's a long shot, but she might know someone."

Kate settled Hannibal into his crate. David was feeling less sore, so he went to put on the prosthetic and walked to his car with two canes.

A small convoy of vehicles set off for the Potlatch Inn. They were joined by Cilla and friends.

Anthony bought the drinks while Kate told them all about Hannibal, and they went outside to look at him. David saw Clair drive in. She glanced over at his group before going inside.

* * *

Ted was playing dominoes. His friend, Jim, was the village taxi driver, a bald guy in his fifties, Summerfield-born, like Ted and May. His wife was in the Oxford Hospital at the same time as May. Now that they were both widowers, they'd become close friends and often met in the Potlatch for a pint of beer.

"It's a nice change from watching TV. Jim likes to play dominoes and cards and neither of us drinks much. It's just nice to be around other people."

* * *

Now Clair sat down with the two of them. "Are you sure you'll only be a few more minutes, guys? I've had a long day."

"Hi Clair, hi guys, may I join you for those few minutes?"

Ted smiled a welcome and David squeezed into the booth beside him and opposite Clair. "Cilla's girlfriends are inquiring about my health, as if I'm being vetted for something."

Clair looked over at Cilla, who was laughing with Kate and Zara.

Jim looked up from the game and laughed. "Sorry, can't talk. I've beaten Ted twice and this is his last chance."

"Are you nervous about the presentation tomorrow?"

"I'll be fine. Your coaching really helped, thank you. But should you be sitting over here with us?"

"Sitting over here with you? What do you mean exactly?"

Clair's throat hurt. The hostile female glares across the room turned to smiles when David followed her gaze.

She gave a short laugh. "You've crossed the line between the Bartlett-Browns and the rest of the village."

She would never be accepted by David's family. He would leave soon, but she would have to go on living in Summerfield.

Ted put down a domino and crowed. "Ha, you weren't expecting that!"

David stood up and looked at Clair with narrowed eyes. "It's only a problem if you live in the past–and I've been away a long time. That old rubbish doesn't apply to me."

Kyle and Gary had come in and now stood at the bar. Kyle's nose was swollen, and his eyes looked 'piggy' with bruising. Both men had unpleasant expressions on their faces as they looked at them.

"Sadly, people have long memories and you're a celebrity now. You just have riding lessons with me.

Please, make it easier, shake hands like a client and go back to your group."

David shrugged and held out his hand. They shook in a business-like manner and then Clair pulled her hand away. She indicated Selena, the landlady, carrying a tray of drinks to Cilla's table. "Your family are being served; it's people like me who do the serving."

Now he frowned. "I can't believe you accept that old stereotype. Everybody serves in one way or another. I'm in the British Army, remember? I've served my country since I was eighteen."

* * *

Back at his table, David was irritable, but Anthony astonished them all. "If Kate will help, I've decided to adopt Hannibal. I can be his foster owner until we can find him a permanent home. That way he won't be euthanized."

Kate shrieked. "You're serious? Oh, I can't thank you enough!" She leaned forward and grasped Anthony's hands between both of hers. "There's a civilian kennels near the Ministry of Defense base and I can teach you all his commands."

Everyone was full of congratulations as they said goodbye. David was aware of Ted and Jim packing up the dominoes, with Clair waiting impatiently by the door.

Kate came back in from the Jeep and sat down beside him. "What a relief! I was steeling myself to say a final goodbye to Hann, but all is well. Anthony and I are meeting in town tomorrow to sort everything out."

She leaned closer and David looked into the blue eyes that went so well with her Celtic brown hair. "I haven't had a chance before this, but I wanted to tell you that I'm leaving the Army. I've been in six years, and since our narrow escape, I've lost my motivation. I was wondering what plans you might have for the future?"

David took her hand and looked at it, gently touching the shrapnel marks that were like his own. In Afghanistan, Kate had wanted to take things to another level but that special spark was not there for him. But she was his friend and deserved his honesty.

"I'm glad, if that's what you want now. But I can't wait to get back to the regiment. It might only be an office role, but it's where I belong. I'm staying in the Army."

* * *

Clair gunned the engine of the Jeep as Ted fastened his seat belt. When they left the pub, David was still holding Kate's hand. She was an attractive woman, with the same background as his, and they looked great sitting together.

Oh well, any warm feelings between them would not survive the feedback tomorrow. Clair slammed the Jeep into reverse and jerked Ted as she turned in a half-circle. She put her foot down hard and they shot across the parking lot. "The Bartlett-Browns so love to dominate everything, don't they?"

"You're not interested in David then?"

Clair stopped at the exit, looked both ways along the road, then pulled out. "He's got enough women interested in him. I've got better things to do."

Chapter 12

David puzzled about the change in Clair. She was not her usual enthusiastic self in his lesson, professional but cool. But he'd pushed himself a bit too hard in a new exercise, felt something tear, and a stab of pain had shot up his thigh. It was a big day tomorrow, as Jack was due to do an assessment. He needed to get home quickly, take painkillers, and soak in a hot tub.

* * *

Clair waited for David on the path and stepped out as he approached. He did not want to stop, but she blocked his way. He glared, "Excuse me, but I need to get home quickly. My leg is extremely painful."

"I'm sorry, but I need to speak with you urgently.

It will only take a minute or two, and it's really important."

His dark eyes were hot with annoyance, but he hesitated. Clair grabbed Ted's old wooden chair and sat down, eye to eye. Steph would make sure no one came this way until she gave the 'all-clear.'

"We agreed to help each other with our goals and we're doing that. I don't want to talk about this other stuff but I'm the only one who can, because you've intimidated everyone else."

David looked down at his thigh and massaged it slowly.

"Your balance is improving every day, and you've had no more attacks of vertigo. We are glad about that, but I'm getting a lot of negative feedback about you from the volunteers."

He shifted uncomfortably in the wheelchair. Was he listening or just waiting for her to stop, so that he could go?

"Firstly, they say you never praise or reward your horse. Winston is a living being, not a train waiting in a station. He listens; but you never talk to him."

David looked furious and burst out impatiently. "I'm not getting better fast enough. My whole life is threatened and it's driving me crazy."

She came straight back at him. "That may be so, but there are other people involved as well as you.

You pay for your lessons, but that only covers the cost of feed and shoes for Winston. Our volunteers put in huge effort without pay, so that your horse is ready for your lesson."

She waited for a reply, but none came. "Our female volunteers say you either ignore them or treat them like military subordinates. They feel you take what is freely given but seem to despise them."

Now David stared blankly at her. He did not look well, and Clair knew she must let him go.

She softened her voice. "We understand you feel angry and vulnerable. But you are wealthy and have everything possible to support your disability. Our challenged youngsters cannot ride unless they are supported by donations and devoted caregivers. You could appreciate the volunteers more and stop wallowing in self-pity."

David bit his lower lip and the lovely feeling between them was gone.

Clair felt tears prickle and forced them back. "Healing with horses is not like lifting weights. There's a quote from someone, I can't remember who, but it's that people and airplanes fly through lift, not push. We want to help you, but the volunteers feel pushed and disrespected."

David's hands locked onto the wheels of his chair.

"Everyone has tough lives David, and they need

help too. It's about taking care of other people and taking care of the horses, as well as yourself."

"Have you finished? I need to go."

He stared pointedly at her until Clair stood up and lifted the chair out of the way. "Thanks for the feedback. I have a behavioral psychologist attached to my case and will be sure to bring this up. I can only apologize for offending your volunteers."

She did not rise to the sarcasm in his tone but watched him as he accelerated to his waiting van. Then she went slowly back to the office.

* * *

It was Patricia's day off. Ted had at last agreed to open his ancient filing cabinet and Sid was sorting old files before they went to Banbury.

He looked up in welcome then his smile disappeared. "Oh dear, what's happened?"

Clair sat down opposite him at the desk and misery came through in her voice. "I just had to give David Brown feedback about his arrogance with our volunteers. That was on top of yesterday, when Steph sent me to check the bottom field. Gary Kidd is so confident of winning that he's bought the fields next to us and started to drain the bottom area."

Clair told him about the heavy machinery. "The

foreman's only in charge of drainage and didn't know what it was for. But he said, from the size of the excavation, it looked like a large building, covering the entire field."

Sid rubbed his chin. "That's worrying, but we have the first presentation this afternoon. Why don't we do half an hour on this, then I'll buy lunch on the way to Banbury. We'll go to the bank and raise some money for the auction."

"Okay." Clair picked up some old envelopes. "At least this is a productive thing to do."

Sid pointed to the two piles of paperwork on the desk. "I'm looking for anything we can use in the fight for the lease. This pile is trash, old feed bills and the like. This other one has things for tax history."

She scanned a document quickly and laid it on the trash pile. "I go over and over it in my head but come up with no answers. If we lose, I've got to settle Granddad somewhere and find another job. At least he still has his pension money from the Estate, to tide us over until I find something."

Sid was focusing intently on the papers in his hand. "Except that he doesn't."

"Excuse me?"

Sid passed her the documents. "Ted cashed in his Estate pension to build the indoor arena for you."

* * *

Clair changed into the smart outfit she'd bought in Oxford and they travelled in Sid's big car. Elegant, black pants were teamed with a crisp, white shirt, short, cropped jacket, and smart, black leather shoes. She had her notes and laptop. Sid, as usual, wore a comfortable tweed suit and had his old, battered briefcase.

Approaching Banbury and looking for a suitable place for lunch, Clair's head suddenly swiveled. "Sid, stop!"

Startled, he looked in his rearview mirror and pulled over. Clair pointed to a small sign with an arrow pointing down a driveway. *KIDD'S CHUNKY CHICKS.*

"Can we just see what the building looks like?"

At the end of the drive they parked in front of a nondescript office block and Clair indicated a road to the side, "You go and chat to the receptionist, and I'll take a look down there."

"I don't think we should ..."

But she opened the door and walked determinedly around the corner.

Behind the offices stood a mammoth warehouse, as big as a football field. A side door was open, and even from where she was standing, the smell of ammonia was overpowering.

Clamping her hand over her nose, Clair went closer and looked in.

Thousands upon thousands of white chickens were packed into the open area, barely able to move. She quickly pulled out her mobile phone and started filming. A minute or so later, a figure in a yellow hazmat suit and helmet appeared at the opposite end of the building and spotted her.

He pulled up his visor. "Hey, what are you doing in here? No visitors allowed."

Clair turned and ran. Sid had not moved and was still sitting in the car, looking unhappy.

She jumped in and they drove back the way they'd come. Clair shuddered. "I've read about intensive chicken farming, but this was worse. There were four more buildings like that one and the back door of that block said, *Research and Development*."

"I still don't think it was a good idea to come here. I should have driven straight on."

But Clair wasn't listening. "The mass market is for chicken legs. Scientific reports say they're trying to breed a chicken with four legs and I bet Gary Kidd will be involved in something like that."

Her stomach heaved and she leaned forward, wrapping her arms around her knees.

Sid glanced anxiously at his watch and drove faster. "You can't say things like that about Gary Kidd or tell anyone that we were here. You have no proof and he'll sue us. Now, you've had nothing to eat before we meet with the Board. I shouldn't have gone down that driveway."

They arrived at the Bank headquarters. "Stay calm, take it slowly and do what you've prepared. I know these folks and there's no pressure."

Inside, they met the committee members and Clair was introduced. With a glance at her pale face, Sid went first with the financials.

But when she stood up, Clair's mind went completely blank. All she could see was the huge barn crammed with white chickens clambering on top of each other and unable to breathe. She could say nothing about Summerfield Stables or the auction. She showed the video of Zach, and Sid closed the session.

They drove away empty-handed.

Clair sat rigid in the passenger seat, near to weeping.

Sid patted her hand. "We crashed and burned on that one. The only thing we can do to sort this situation is to keep trying to raise money and win the auction. We'll do better next time."

Chapter 13

Clair came in with puffy eyelids next morning and did not want to talk about what had happened at the presentation. Luckily, Patricia was watching Ted in the arena. He was driving the small tractor with the back rake around and around, smoothing the sand before lessons.

"It's good to have him back again."

Clair had come in to grab another cup of coffee before she had to teach. She held onto it with both hands. "I need to cut back on the caffeine, not have more, but yeah, even with everything hanging over us, Granddad's almost back to his old self."

Patricia turned and smiled. "Which is more than you can say for Kyle's nose!"

Clair leaned against the desk sipping the coffee. "I despise that man. We were working on my presentation after class, then Kyle turned up and polluted the air with his crude remarks."

She moved her shoulders to ease the stiffness, trying to pretend the ache was Kyle. But David had not returned after her negative feedback. "He's told people that David broke his nose because of me. David's expected to date all the women in Summerfield, but I'm despised for being seen with him."

Patricia moved her chair up to the computer. "Anyone who knows you understands what Kyle's up to. If you enjoy being with David, why do you care what other people think?"

Clair gazed at her. "I wish it were that simple. David's going back to the Army, but I'll still be here, coping with village life. Maybe, he's gone already? He didn't come for his lesson and the Sponsored Ride is this afternoon."

"I don't think David would leave without saying goodbye."

"He agreed to be a Roman soldier with Robert in the Nativity production, so I hope he comes back for that."

Patricia started on emails and Clair finished her coffee. She wanted to see David as passionately as she wished Kyle was on the other side of the planet. Both seemed unrealistic, so she went back to work.

* * *

David, meanwhile, was in Jack's car and nearing London. Jack was driving and David was thinking about Clair. He pictured her again on that rainy night at college, standing up tall from under the hood of her old Jeep, her eyes flashing angrily. Now he was angry with her and humiliated by the feedback.

In the back of the car, two Regimental dress uniforms swung on coat hangers, buttons polished, and pants with knife-edge creases. David's prosthetic now had an interchangeable foot for different shoes and two pairs of boots were on the floor behind the seats. They were polished, so that faces reflected in them.

"I'm glad you shaved off that beard." Jack eased into the stream of traffic on the motorway. "I was anticipating what the Sergeant-Major would say to greet you when he saw it"

David laughed. "Yeah, some choice language, I'm sure. Thanks for driving me today. I'm determined to walk to get my medal, but I'm still a bit shaky."

"I'm sure you'll be fine, but I'll be right behind you with the chair if you need it."

Jack found some music they both liked on the radio and soon after that, they entered the London suburbs. David had an appointment with his physical therapist before lunch.

* * *

Finn watched him take off the prosthetic leg and examined his stump. "Some minor tearing, but most of the skin grafts are intact and healing well. This is unbelievable, compared to last time! What changed?"

"I'm taking your advice at last. I'm training more carefully and having therapeutic riding lessons for the vertigo."

Clair came into his mind again, not the embarrassment and anger he'd been feeling, but the freckles on her nose.

"David?"

"What? Sorry, sorry, I was miles away. I only use the wheelchair when I'm exhausted."

"Okay, put the prosthetic back on and let's see what you can do."

In t-shirt and shorts, David completed the circuit of exercises, breathless but happy with his times. Finn applauded. "I think you're ready for the titanium leg."

"Brilliant!"

Finn went into the storeroom to fetch the new

prosthetic. He had a naturally positive personality and probably related well to all his clients. Like Clair.

"It's one of our newest innovations." Finn fitted him with the titanium prosthetic and sat down at the desk. "The robotic knee should make horse riding easier. But it's still in development so we'd like to know how it performs." He tapped a command into the laptop and David jerked, "Hey!"

He grinned as Finn passed him a hand controller. "Send it instructions very slowly. Walk around for a bit, then try the stairs again."

David came down the stair unit, holding tightly to the rail. "Easier to go up than come down, but it's amazing. I feel almost normal."

But when he took the new prosthetic off, the scar tissue was bruised. "I didn't even feel that happening."

Finn applied a dressing. "Wear the old one today and take the titanium leg home to practice. Call me with any problems and I'll see you in a month."

* * *

Mrs. Jessop had made them an amazing packed lunch, which they ate sitting in Jack's car. They changed into dress uniforms at the clinic and Jack then drove to the Parade Ground.

David wheeled ahead into the tent for Medal recipients and the air was suddenly blue with jokes and raucous laughter! It was great to have a big catch-up with veterans from Rehab, before they were called to take their places for the ceremony.

A chilly wind blew across the tarmac. David spotted Anthony and Cilla among the other families and they waved.

"Good of them to come."

"They're very proud of you."

Jack stood to attention beside David's wheelchair as the band turned onto the square, playing the Regimental march. The Colonel-in-Chief ascended the stage to take the salute.

Rank upon rank of soldiers marched past the podium and the crash of boots in perfect time were part of the music. There was a lump in David's throat. He was a soldier. These men and women were his extended family.

"Captain David Bartlett-Brown."

Walking steadily, David reached the stage and transferred both canes to his left hand. He saluted smartly, received his combat medal, and walked back to his place. Jack was several paces behind him with the wheelchair.

"Congratulations!"

Anthony and Cilla met him in the refreshment

tent and David introduced them to his colleagues.

The Commanding Officer approached, and everyone saluted. He shook hands all around, then turned to David. "Many congratulations on your medal, Captain."

"Thank you, Sir."

The others faded quietly away as the CO sat down next to him and took a business card from his breast pocket. "Thank you for your application to my office." He handed him the card. "There are several opportunities open for someone with your expertise. Give me a call when Major Harris signs you off."

The CO left him to speak with others and David stared down at the card.

Driving home later, Jack chatted about the day. "A total success; and a titanium leg will make teaching at the Oxford College easier. The Administrator called to ask if you were interested in a full-time job."

"It was a useful fill-in, so thanks for setting it up; but the CO gave me his card. I'll be returning to the Regiment as soon as you sign me off."

David reclined the seat to ease the pressure on his leg and Clair came into his mind again. Once he was back into Army life again, Clair and Summerfield would be left behind. He realized now that her feedback was a wake-up call for him. Riding lessons had helped his vertigo, but he'd become isolated and self-centered. He could change that. He'd go to the Stables early tomorrow and be more sociable. The future lay in his pocket with a Regimental business card.

Chapter 14

Patricia answered the phone. "Okay, I'll tell her."

Clair stopped what she was doing at the tone of Patricia's voice. "More bad news? It's all we seem to get lately."

"That was my friend from the deli. Someone just came in from the market and said the lease had been sold, prior to auction."

Clair grabbed her mobile and scrolled through her messages. "There's nothing here. Sold prior to the auction? Surely that's not possible?"

She jumped up and grabbed her jacket. "Steph's free. Could you ask Robert to cover for me in the next lesson? We'll go to the Land Agent's office and see what's going on."

It was market day in Summerfield.

Clair and Steph pushed between the stalls and

people buying vegetables. "I wish Lizzie were still here; I loved her artisan bread."

There was a small crowd by the steps leading to the offices of Ogilvy and Ogilvy. They said hi to several people, but before they could discuss the rumors, Steph nudged Clair.

Cilla Bartlett-Brown had come out of her equestrian boutique on the opposite side of the street with a face like thunder. Clair was curiously relieved that it was not David's sister sabotaging the auction.

Quentin Ogilvy came out of his office and stood at the top of the steps, looking down on them and Clair called up, "Quentin, we've heard the Stables lease has been sold before the auction. Is that true?"

He smiled pleasantly, as if it was no big deal. "Yes, that is correct. We received a high offer, and it's been accepted."

"Surely it's not legal to terminate an auction? Why weren't we all given the chance to make offers?"

Quentin raised his eyebrows and adjusted his burgundy satin vest. "If you cared to do your research before making accusations, it's perfectly legal. Ogilvy and Ogilvy represent the interests of the Duke, and the lease to Summerfield Stables is sold."

Cilla's voice rose above the others. "Just a minute, Quentin."

Everybody fell back as she stalked through and fixed him with a beady eye. "The Duke is a close friend of my family. I'm going to call him right now and see what he has to say about this."

Her voice had a *I-don't-take-any-nonsense-from-the-likes-of-you* edge to it as she pulled out her cell phone. "It may be legal to sell a lease before auction, but it's not ethical–and I suspect the Duke knows nothing about it."

Quentin looked nervous. Ignoring his bluster, she marched up the steps and into his office. He hurried after her.

Clair laughed. "I almost feel sorry for poor Quentin."

Steph shook her head vehemently. "Nah, that one deserves everything he gets."

Conversations buzzed.

A few minutes later, Cilla reappeared. She looked down on them from the top of the steps in an almost friendly way. "An offer has been received by the Duke's Agent, but the Duke has *not* accepted it. He understands the situation better now, and the auction will go ahead as advertised."

People cheered as Cilla came down and paused next to Clair. "Make no mistake, I intend to win the auction. But my family doesn't need to cheat."

Steph marveled as they walked back to the Jeep.

"Fancy her being on the same side as us–like, ever!"

Clair recalled something David said at the River Inn. "Apparently, she had a lot of responsibility and was left to look after David when they were young. She developed a thick skin. Maybe we could have been friends in different circumstances?"

Back at the Stables, everyone gathered in the Training Room to hear what happened. Patricia popped her head around the door and beckoned to Clair. "He's back."

* * *

David had driven himself to his lesson to arrive an hour early and brought a juicy apple for Winston. Palming chunks under the long muzzle, he felt gentle lips and warm breath on his hand. It was nice and he talked softly to him for a while. Some of the female volunteers were tacking up ponies. He saw now how much they did and how much the Stables depended on them. He made eye contact and smiled. "Hi! Does anyone know if I could watch Clair teach a lesson?"

Someone pointed to Steph walking between the stalls behind him. "I'm on my break so that I can watch Nick in Clair's class. Come up to the Viewing Room with us."

The narrow staircase was still too difficult for his prosthetic, so David took the wheelchair elevator. As the doors opened at the top, he saw the whole arena spread below them through a darkened picture window.

Steph introduced him to the other mums and caregivers. David grinned at them and noticed they all had cups of coffee from the vending machine. He tried to get one, but it was difficult to manage with his canes. Someone offered to carry his cup to the table for him. Usually standoffish and irritable, David thanked her gratefully and noticed the women nodding between themselves. Heat tingled in his face. He'd been such a pain; but he hoped they saw he was trying harder.

Below them, Robert mounted three students with the hoist while Clair was preparing equipment for the class. There were four youngsters and eight volunteer helpers.

"Two volunteers to each student is our normal ratio," Steph explained to him. "It's three-to-one with severely challenged youngsters."

David was rueful. "They handle that hoist better than I did." Clair's positive energy talking with the youngsters was magnetic and he could not take his eyes off her.

Steph grinned at him slyly. "Fascinating, isn't

she? We also notice, if anyone mentions your name, Clair lights up like a Christmas tree."

Before he could ask her to elaborate, there came an agonized howl from the arena. Nick was suspended in the air, crying and fighting the harness.

Steph was out of her chair and running. Through the big window, they watched Robert lower Nick slowly back into his wheelchair. Steph appeared and leaped onto the ramp. She unstrapped the harness, talking reassuringly, turned his wheelchair and headed out to the transport vans. Nick was still screaming and lashing out in all directions.

David turned to the others. "I don't understand– what happened?"

"The ponies all have weight limits," a friend of Steph's pointed to the hoist, "The weight of each student is recorded. Today, Nick tipped the scales; he's too heavy for Teddy and there's no other pony suitable for his ability."

"But what will he do if he can't ride anymore?"

She stared at him as if he was stupid. "If Clair loses the lease, what will any of us do?"

* * *

Back in the arena, things were calm again. Clair led a game where the volunteers helped their youngsters select a colored hoop, ride across the arena, put it over a post, then go back for another. They were being monitored for safety, but also encouraged to race. There were giggles and excited grins under the crash helmets.

In a fifteen-minute lesson, Clair managed it so there was fun, laughter, and that every child won a rosette.

After the 'high fives,' the caregivers took over and Clair ran lightly up the stairs. "Hi! They said you were up here. It's good to see you."

David knew she did not hold a grudge like Cilla did. Why had he felt so nervous?

"You're in a mixed class today, and I think you'll enjoy it."

David wrinkled his nose. He'd rather be on his own with her but thinking of the feedback, he said nothing. Robert supervised mounting with seven members of the group. Wearing his new prosthetic David could now mount Winston with just Robert to support him.

Clair showed them a huge iron key that was hung on a cord around her neck. "It's a bit chilly, but such a beautiful day that we're going into the Duke's private park. When Ted was Head Coachman, the back gate was his route to take horses and carriages to the Mansion. After he retired, we still had the privilege of riding there. But sadly, the current Duke is having the gate walled up, so we'll take this opportunity for a ride before it's gone."

* * *

There was the pad and slither of hooves in the mud, as they moved under the tunnel of bare trees. Clair thought back over the many times they'd used this track and the glorious views over the park.

Robert walked at the front, leading the ride. She checked in with all the riders and volunteers. Everyone was doing well, so she settled at the back as rear marker.

David chatted with another rider and was riding confidently on Winston. He looked back to see where she was, then reined Winston in, allowing others to pass.

He grinned when Clair reached him. "Hey, how are you doing back here?"

"I'm good, thank you." She smiled up at him, thinking how handsome he was. She patted Winston's neck and walked along next to him. "Did Cilla tell you that she put Quentin Ogilvy in his place?"

David threw back his head and laughed. "Yeah! Cilla can be formidable, but it sounded like he deserved it. I'm still confused about her feud with you and the Stables, didn't she help you at one time?"

"Her dressage group hired the arena regularly, but that was before the difficulties with the hayfields."

He nodded, as if he'd heard about that. "She told me that you discriminated against her."

Clair responded firmly to that. "We did not discriminate. We had no choice, because she refused to pay for the grazing. Zara has plenty of land around Woodstock; Cilla just doesn't like driving over there."

Robert had reached the point where two paths crossed and called back down the line. "Which way?"

"Left, away from the Kidd earthworks."

"Good choice."

The horses moved on and everyone seemed pleased to be out in the open air. There were glimpses of the park but they were nearing the point to turn around.

"Cilla can be bossy, I grant you, but I've needed her help."

"I understand that, of course. But she's been unreasonable. It makes me mad that she wants to destroy our work."

"I want to continue riding with you." He grinned

down at her from Winston's broad back. "Or haven't you noticed the change in my behavior? You told me to mind my manners with your volunteers or find myself somewhere else to ride. So, I'm minding my manners!"

Clair laughed and the tension was broken.

* * *

David breathed in the scent of leaf-mold and looked up at the blue sky above them. Winston's ears flicked backward and forward, as if listening to the birdsong. David heaved a sigh and counted his blessings.

Then, there was a barrage of gunfire.

All the horses startled but he slumped over Winston's neck as if he'd been shot. Clair leaped to grab the bridle and pushed his left heel down, to keep his foot in the stirrup.

He heard her voice in the far distance. "David, you're okay. People are shooting rabbits on the far side of the wood. I'm going to take your hand now and guide it to Winston's mane."

David fought the vertigo, trying not to vomit.

"Can you feel how solid he is? I need you to breathe deeply and slowly, in case the shooting starts again. Say yes, if you can hear me."

Robert come in on the other side and he felt his prosthetic leg pressed against the saddle. "Good boy, Winston. Remember that he was in a riot, David, but he's calm, and there's no danger now. Clair and I are both here with you and you're not going to fall. Try and take deep breaths now."

David shuddered, the sweat beading on his forehead. But slowly he opened his eyes. "Sorry, guys ... sorry."

The volunteers had turned all the horses, and everyone waited quietly.

Robert looked up at him. "Anyone who went through what you did would have lost it then. You didn't fall off and you came back to us quickly. I think you're almost well again."

* * *

At the bank presentation later that afternoon, Clair and Sid were in perfect harmony.

Clair began with the video of Zach and covered all the coaching points from sessions with David. On the big screen, their beloved ponies gave her courage.

"Thank you so much for seeing us today." Clair smiled and made eye contact with Board members. "The children who ride with us have disabilities which limit their lives. But over and over again, we see that being with horses and ponies reduces trauma. Our students forget their challenges for a while and find serenity in the company of a horse."

Clair clicked to the slideshow. On the screen, a cavalcade of children passed by, smiling down at the camera from their ponies. "The booklet in front of you has testimonials from parents and caregivers. But Sid has shown you that we walk a financial tightrope. Owning the lease, we can continue to provide quality riding experiences for able-bodied youngsters, at a competitive price. We can then use that income to fund equine therapy for people with challenges."

Clair paused, trying to communicate how deeply she cared. "To win the lease at auction and secure the future of Summerfield Stables, we desperately need your help."

She waited in the hallway, pacing up and down until Sid came out, beaming.

"I knew you could do it. They granted us £100,000!"

Clair flung her arms around him in an enormous hug. "Oh, Sid! I never could have done this without you. How many more could we do before Christmas?"

Chapter 15

Cilla caught David before he could reach the front door. "I thought you said you were staying neutral. I just heard you were at the River Inn with Clair Williams and broke her boyfriend's nose. Doesn't sound very neutral to me!"

"The village grapevine knows everything, but it's not always accurate, is it? Clair is one of my college students and Kyle Sanders insulted me. Bullies thrive when you don't defend yourself, so I defended myself."

"I don't expect he liked seeing his girlfriend with you."

David didn't reply. Clair was not Kyle's girlfriend, but Cilla liked to fish for gossip.

"Clair Williams is bidding against us and we've

always said that family is more important than anything. You are over at the Stables all the time."

David yearned for the freedom of his Army life.

"I told you about our Commanding Officer giving me his card at the Medal ceremony?"

Cilla nodded.

"The interviews are in early January and I need Jack to sign me off. The final test is the Nativity Ride, in which I'm a Roman soldier with Robert. Being bad guys, we are riding the two black horses. I'm on Rebel, who is a more spirited ride than Winston."

He sighed at the lack of comprehension on Cilla's face. "Robert rarely rides because of his back injury, so he needs the quieter horse. We enter at the canter and I'm trying not to fall off. So far, Rebel's run away with me twice."

"Oh, well, okay then. But are you back for dinner tonight? You could go over my plans for the Stables with me."

"After rehearsals, we're watching the European soccer Semi-Final match."

David felt marginally guilty, coupling Robert with the soccer match. He intended to watch the game with Ted and hoped to make an Italian dinner for him and Clair. Since the vertigo attack in the woods, he was increasingly drawn to her warmth and kindness. He'd ask her for a date; but he was too close to returning to the Army and leaving Summerfield for good.

David opened the front door. "You don't need me to go over anything with you. You know what you want, and you usually get it."

Cilla smiled. "You're right, of course. I always win, when I put my mind to it. Don't forget drinks and nibbles at the boutique tomorrow night, please. When I win the lease, we'll buy a safe horse for you and we can ride out together."

She studied herself in the hall mirror, tidying a strand of hair. "I've decided to go on living here after the auction. It's much more comfortable than that musty-smelling old cottage. But someone needs to be there at night. I was thinking that Clair Williams could manage the place for me. What do you think?"

He snapped at her as he headed out to his car. "For goodness sake, Cilla! Why should I know or care? Clair's a buddy, like Jack and the guys from the Regiment. We don't discuss stuff like that."

Cilla followed him. "I still wish you'd come out with my group occasionally. You used to be so sociable and Zara's seriously interested in you."

David started the engine. "I wish you'd stop interfering. My gratitude for your help doesn't extend to dating your friends."

"But Zara would be a good match for you, you know. Why not take her to the Regimental Dinner?"

David snorted and put the Jag into gear. "Zara wants the dashing officer I used to be, not a damaged veteran with a prosthetic leg."

"What about taking your friend Kate then? I'm in London for the weekend of the dinner so I can't go with you. You need to be out in public again and with a Bartlett-Brown sort of girl."

"'Bye, Cilla. It's all irrelevant anyway, because I'm not going to the Regimental Dinner."

* * *

David chatted with Robert as they untacked Rebel and Blackbird after rehearsal. It was Friday, 5:00 p.m. and when he took Rebel's saddle to the Tack Room, a small group of volunteers were working. They stopped chatting when they saw him in the doorway.

Steph smiled and moved Nick's wheelchair a bit then beckoned him in. "Come and help us?"

David grinned at Nick, grabbed a chair and sat down next to him. He dismantled a bridle at top speed and laughed at the incredulous faces. "We do a lot of this sort of thing in the Army, guys."

Clair came in with Rebel's bridle. "Oh dear,

somebody gave this horse a treat with the bit still in his mouth."

She knew it was David but pretended to scold whoever it was. "I don't expect his rider knew, but this bit must be rinsed in cold water before the bridle is hung up."

"Yes, ma'am."

Everyone giggled as she went out.

Work began again and conversations started up.

"My dad says you were in Afghanistan on a secret mission."

David recognized Maddie from the jumping competition. "Your dad is correct about Afghanistan, but it wasn't secret. I was helping to set up schools and health clinics, I trained Afghani Army officers."

Nick was carefully polishing a saddle with Maddie. "I'm going to ride in the Paralympics one day."

Robert had told David about the degenerative condition that would confine Nick to a wheelchair for life. Thinking back to the explosion, David knew now that he'd been lucky.

The chimes of the Summerfield mobile fish and chip shop sounded outside, and Nick turned his wheelchair from the table. "Yay!"

He headed for the elevator and Maddie hurried

after him. David helped Steph put the saddle soap and sponges away.

"Maddie lives near us in the village and helps with me with Nick."

"She seems a very nice girl." He hesitated. "Okay, I'll be off now."

"You could stay, if you wanted. You've been helping a lot lately, and we only get a treat dinner once a month."

"Okay, thanks!"

Steph went to tell Clair that David was staying. He waited in line for the elevator and soon Clair came in, her arms full of bundles.

"Hey! Granddad said you might be making pasta tonight, but he and Robert are joining us as well. Nothing so English as the smell of a fish dinner and fries creeping through newspaper, is there? I'll keep yours wrapped until you get there."

When the elevator doors opened, David saw that tables had been pushed together, with chairs and wheelchairs around them. Steph and Robert came up the stairs with Ted, and Clair passed out the fish dinners.

"Thanks for all your help, everyone. This is on the Stables account, so dig in!"

Nick squirted tomato ketchup on his fries and passed the bottle to David. "This is my totally favorite dinner." He picked out the fish, then ate the batter. "But I don't like the white bit in the middle."

David caught Steph's eye. She was about to tell Nick to eat the only nutritious part of the fish and chips. "Need to pick your battles, eh, mum?"

They both laughed and turned back to their own dinners. It was such an easy atmosphere, with everyone talking and eating together.

After they cleared up, David hung back as people said goodnight.

Ted called back as he went down the stairs. "See you at the cottage. I'll get the TV warmed up."

There was a soft expression in Clair's eyes as she sat down and indicated he should join her. "You wanted to ask me something?"

"Yes, about being a financial buddy for Nick. Anthony, Cilla, and I were fortunate to have Trust Funds from our father. I bought an apartment in London with mine and I sponsor a school in Afghanistan. Robert says Nick desperately needs a mobile hoist. I can afford to pay for that. Do you know where we could order one?

"I do, and it would be an incredible help to them. There used to be government funding, but it stopped, and Steph struggles to manage."

David was watching her face and suddenly wondered if he had offered to help Nick because of her? No. His conscience told him that he genuinely wanted to give something back for the gift of his survival. Nick was closer to home but as much in need as kids in Afghanistan. "Could we keep it between ourselves?"

She nodded, "Of course. Patricia does the ordering but she's very discreet, and we'll tell Steph it's from an anonymous donor."

"Okay, start with the hoist and we could talk about other things later."

"That's fantastic! I hope you won't mind me asking, but Nick was disappointed when you didn't come to the Sponsored Ride. Was there a reason that I could share with him?"

"I'm sorry about that and I'll tell him myself when I see him tomorrow. I needed to be in London that day, at the Medal Ceremony for Afghanistan."

* * *

The cottage was full of the fragrance of coffee, and Jossie wriggled to meet them.

"Smells good, Ted. Hope it's decaf or I'll be awake all night!"

"It is. Twenty minutes till the kick-off."

They sat chatting at the kitchen table and David leaned down to stroke Jossie. "I was thinking, if

Nick can't ride Teddy, is there a way we could adapt his special saddle to the pony cart? Robert told me you hire it out for weddings sometimes. Could Nick learn to drive it?"

Clair beamed. "What an inspired idea! If it worked, he would have a whole new focus."

No one mentioned that they might not be there, and Ted reached for his cane. "Stay there, I want to show you something."

When he was out of earshot, rummaging in his room, David leaned in and spoke softly, "I'm embarrassed to repeat this, but Cilla said something which might be helpful at a later date."

A minute or so later, Ted came back holding the TV remote and an old photograph album. He laid both carefully on the table. "They're still interviewing people before the match, so take a look at a bit of history."

Clair recognized the faded red cover of the album and reached out a gentle hand to touch it. "I haven't seen this for years. I used to love looking through it with Grandma May."

Ted sat down and found a picture of two huge horses. Between them was a man in working clothes, his breeches tied under the knee.

"That's my Dad. See the string under his knees?

There were big rats in the barns; string stopped them from running up your legs."

Clair shuddered and came around the table to see more clearly. She leaned over the back of Ted's chair, and David caught the scent of coconut. He tried not to stare at the exquisite curve of her lips. Her hand rested on her Grandfather's shoulder as she smiled down at the photos.

"That's you, up there, isn't it? How old are you?"

High on one of the giant work horses, a small boy grinned from ear to ear. "Seven or eight, and I went everywhere with my dad. He loved horses, and when I was growing up, we used them for everything. These two are the old Duke's prize Clydesdales, strong enough to haul big carts, with hooves the size of dinner plates. But this is what I wanted to show you."

Ted turned the page. "I was fifteen and so proud to be driving her Ladyship in the pony cart. If you and Robert can make that saddle fit, David, I'll teach Nick to drive."

From the room next door, the announcer named the players as they ran onto the field and Ted picked up the remote, "Let's go! I hope we get a better referee this time."

"Just before that, can I show you something too?"

David lifted the right leg of his jeans a little to

reveal a matt silver shaft, with a foot that matched his designer running shoes. "State-of-the-art, high-tech titanium. It's all mine and hot to trot. If things go well at the Nativity Ride, Jack says he'll sign me off to return to work."

Ted and Clair stared at the leg, then Ted clapped him on the shoulder. "Well, I'm impressed."

David smiled as he shook the leg of his jeans back into place. "You should be, Ted. As a British taxpayer, you paid for it. But watch out, waving that TV remote around, or I'll end up out in the yard!"

* * *

Clair watched them go, laughing and then settling to watch the soccer match. She pulled the old photo album closer, turning to the page with the sepia snapshots of May and Ted's wedding. Then she turned all the pages slowly and thought about what David had told her.

If Cilla won the lease, could she possibly take the job of managing the Stables for her? It would be Cilla's final revenge and Clair's soul shrank at the very thought. But would she do it, if it meant Ted could stay in his home? Or in the hope that David might visit his sister from time to time?

Chapter 16

Only a week until the end of the working year and Clair was on a high. All the banks and companies in the Oxford area had been successfully covered and today they'd been further afield. On the way home Clair stopped to have dinner with Sid and Viv.

Viv was Lizzie's aunt and had known Clair all the years she and Lizzie were growing up in Summerfield. Viv now looked after Lizzie's mum, her sister, Christine, who was in a dementia home nearby.

"I haven't seen you in SO long!" She pulled Clair into a warm hug. "Come in and let me take your coat. You look very smart and Sid says you've done amazingly well in all the presentations. I want to hear all about it and what's going on at the Stables. I see Patricia occasionally, but she doesn't gossip.

Anything that doesn't have numbers, as you know, goes straight over Sid's head!"

She led the way to the warm family room, which smelled of good cooking. Viv reminded Clair of Lizzie, with her soft, blond hair and similar figure. Viv and Lizzie also shared a love of cooking, and Clair was ravenous after the presentation. She squatted down to greet Pluto, the sire of Jester.

"Hello, lovely boy."

The old black Labrador thumped his tail but did not move from his basket. Clair stroked his head, looking with love into his milky eyes. Viv and Sid had taken both dogs when Lizzie moved to Scotland. But after a disastrous few weeks, they asked her to find a new home for Jester.

Clair looked up at Viv. "The only positive thing I can say about Kyle Sanders is that he's trained Jester well. How's Pluto doing?"

Viv had donned padded oven gloves and was carrying a big covered casserole dish to the table. "Not bad for an incredibly old dog. He's almost blind with cataracts, but he still enjoys his food and short walks. We'll hang on until he's ready to go."

She opened the door to the hallway and called, "Sid, I'm serving up."

There was a muffled shout from upstairs. "Would

you like to use the downstairs bathroom? Then dinner will be ready."

Clair had brought casual sweatpants, a top, and casual shoes. She changed from her formal clothes and accepted a glass of wine. "Just the one because I'm driving, but it's exactly what I need. Cheers!"

Sid came downstairs, now changed out of his business suit and looking comfortable in jeans and sweatshirt. Viv was younger than Sid and still worked at an Oxford college.

Eating delicious food with old friends, Clair relaxed and caught up on all their news. "Everything has been so busy that Lizzie and I only manage an occasional call. Are they here over the holiday?"

"They just left for Christmas in the US with Dan and Jenna, plus Harry's mum, and Greg. But they're back in mid-January and stopping here to see us and Christine. I'll give you a call when I know their dates."

"Is there any improvement in Christine?"

Viv shook her head and Sid reached out to squeeze her hand. "It's all downhill. One of us goes every day, but Chris doesn't recognize us anymore. We used to take Pluto and she liked that, but she's not unhappy and we're grateful for small mercies. Patricia says Ted's back on form."

"And what a relief that is!"

Viv and Patricia had worked together at the same college and it was on Viv's recommendation that Patricia joined the Stables.

After dessert, which was Viv's spectacular Pavlova, Clair stretched and glanced at her watch. "Oops, time flies! Thank you for that beautiful dinner, but I'm due to pick up Granddad from the Potlatch."

Clair drove home with extra care. She crept slowly along the main street of Summerfield village, watching out for cats and foxes. Cilla's boutique was aglow with Christmas lights and several people were just going in. There were balloons and streamers in the window.

Clair turned into the dark parking lot that was usually crowded with market stalls. Switching off her lights and engine, she could now hear the music. Was David there?

Of course.

He stood near a window, handsome in well-cut black slacks and a white, silk, turtleneck shirt. He was chatting with Kate and Zara, both wearing glittering evening attire. Clair pulled ruefully at her baggy sweats. The women all looked gorgeous and David was inside, while she was outside, looking in.

Resenting the burn of jealousy in her chest, Clair started the engine again and slid quietly back onto the road. There was a bright moon, so she did not turn on the headlights until she was clear of the boutique. Then Clair smiled.

She faced the fact that she didn't have the connections or the clothes to be one of Cilla and David's social set. But she was different and unique. Did she really want to fit in with them?

At the opposite end of the High Street was the Potlatch Inn. Warm light from the windows splashed over grey stone and Selena had filled the hanging baskets with holly and red poinsettias. The old wooden sign, a potlatch boulder on a green field, was decorated too. Clair felt happy to be here and not at Cilla's party.

Even better, neither Kyle nor Gary Kidd were in the pub. Clair gave Ted a kiss on the cheek and smiled at Jim.

Ted looked up from his hand of cards. "Did you have a good time with Viv and Sid?"

"I did, and they sent you their best. No hurry, I'll have a soda before we go."

At the bar, next to the booth with Ted and Jim, people were discussing the auction. "There'll be little change of use, if Cilla Bartlett-Brown gets it."

"Only that ordinary folk and disabled kids won't be able to ride there anymore."

Clair said hi to Selena and ordered a tonic water with ice and lemon.

"Gary Kidd will bring jobs to the village; people eat a lot of chicken."

Ted knew the young man who spoke and joined in the conversation, "When I was growing up, we didn't have meat every day. We ate roast on Sunday, cold cuts on Monday, maybe leftovers in a pie on Tuesday, then vegetables and Yorkshire puddings for the rest of the week. We respected our animals by eating everything, including the liver and kidneys. Delicious and full of nutrition."

Several young people stared at him as he laid a card. Then one of the girls wrinkled her nose. "Eeeeww!"

They all roared with laughter, so Clair jumped in. "Fried chicken legs are heavily processed with fat, sugar, and salt. And they're expensive."

A girl shrugged. "Most families around here eat takeout food. Are you a vegetarian? We can't all afford organic, you know."

"I'm not vegetarian, but I've cut down on meat. It's either our own chicken or organic now. I'm passionate that animals be kept in decent conditions, not exploited for bigger profits. Look at this."

She turned on her phone and held it up so they could all see the screen. "Gary Kidd says chicken welfare is his top priority. But this is a clip from local TV news, after he'd been prosecuted for keeping chickens in terrible conditions. He got a massive fine."

On the small screen, Gary was being interviewed outside the Court House, "This is fake news. I doubt the videos were from our farm."

Clair clicked her phone again and ran the footage she'd shot in Banbury. "I filmed this last week, at his factory, not ten miles from here."

People craned their necks and saw the vast barn, packed wall to wall with white chickens, struggling to stand and breathe.

Clair wanted them to care so much that she almost pleaded, "Donate to the Stables fund and stop him from doing this in Summerfield."

But people turned away, not wanting to be involved.

Ted looked sympathetic as she clicked off the phone. "They have to make up their own minds. But don't worry, if we lose the lease, something else will turn up."

Jim was impatient. "Ted, are you playing cards, or what?"

Ted grinned at Clair and she turned back to the bar with her soda, just as Steph came in. "Hi, did the presentation go well?"

"It did! We got grants from both companies. I'll report back in the meeting tomorrow but I'm too tired to talk about it now. How's Nick?"

Steph hopped up onto the bar stool beside her and ordered a light beer.

"Great news! The mobile hoist arrived, and we got him to bed on time. Mum's there now and told me to slip out for a break."

She sipped the beer appreciatively. "Mmm… the hoist means we can spend Christmas with my sister. We haven't been able to do that since Nick was little and he's totally excited about seeing his cousins. But he's got this hero-worship thing for David now, which is seriously annoying me. It's 'David says this' and 'David says that.' Huh!"

Clair's shoulders sagged a little. She longed to tell Steph that David had paid for Nick's hoist, but she just sipped her soda.

"He'll be gone soon. Everyone's stressed about the auction, so we need to stay positive for our youngsters and the volunteers."

Steph was relaxing now. "Yeah, you're right. But I need to tell you, if we lose the lease to Gary, there's so little opportunity around here, I'll be forced to work at the chicken farm."

* * *

When they arrived home, Ted went straight indoors, out of the cold, and Clair took Jossie for a quick walk. She was not pleased when Gary Kidd's flashy car swept into the empty parking lot.

He stalked over to her, looking around to see if anyone else was there. "I want to speak to you, confidentially."

Clair pointed up at the lighted windows above Reception. "Robert can hear if I shout, but the horses don't talk to anyone much. What do you want?"

"You need to stop pestering people with your crackpot ideas and bad-mouthing me. I could prosecute–but if you shut up now, when I get the lease, I'll buy the arena from you."

Gary mentioned a sum of money and Clair looked at him with narrowed eyes. "We both know that's three times what it cost to build."

He shrugged. "I've got the money and I want this place. People in the village are supporting me and I'll outbid everyone at the auction. A free-range chicken farm will generate income for Summerfield."

"That's sales talk and you know it. It won't be free-range. You're having the foundations dug for another chicken factory at the bottom of our fields."

Gary's face turned ugly and Clair took a step

backward. She looked around for Jossie. Should she shout for Robert?

But he forced a smile. "That building will be a state-of-the-art research and processing facility. If you don't oppose me or drag up any more media stuff, then I'll buy the arena. What do you say?"

Clair wanted to tell him where to stick his money. But if he did win, they could replace Granddad's pension fund.

"It's not my decision to make. I'll put your offer to my grandfather."

"You've got twenty-four hours, or no deal."

Gary roared his car through the gate and Clair went to find Ted.

He was in his room and screwed his face up in disgust when she told him of Gary's offer. "You know what your Grandma would say? 'Get thee behind me, Satan,' that's what."

He struggled to get out of his easy chair and stomped out into the kitchen. "If he wins the auction, he'll deny he ever made such an offer. You keep doing presentations and give us a chance to win that lease. If we lie down with dirty dogs like Gary Kidd, we'll just end up with fleas."

Chapter 17

At the staff meeting, Sid complimented Clair on her excellent presentations, but would not say how much was in the fund.

Steph protested, "If we knew how much we'd raised, wouldn't it motivate people for a last push?"

"It might, but it would also alert the competition. Clair and I have four more meetings with companies, then there's the collection at the Nativity Ride. But we still need to stay confidential until the auction. Okay, I'm off to confirm those meetings now."

As Sid gathered his things and left, Robert smiled at Clair and stood up with Steph.

"We're covering all your stable duties until you finish the presentations and rehearsals."

She sighed with relief. "Thank you, guys, that will help such a lot."

He and Steph went back to the yard and Sophie, Patricia's dog, came out from under the table.

Patricia bent to pat her. "Good girl, we'll be going home soon. Clair, I'm coming in every day until we break for Christmas to coordinate choir practices. Why don't you delegate everything except rehearsals to me until the Nativity Ride?"

Clair felt the itch of tears and rubbed her eyes. "I have such a great team and you're an absolute gem. We *must* win at the auction, but I know people are making plans, in case we lose, because I'm having to think about that too."

Patricia opened the door to let Sophie into the yard. "It's natural when there might be radical change. But whatever the outcome, you know already that my training to be verger for St. Peter's starts in January."

Clair bit her lower lip because she had forgotten. Patricia's main passion was to get St Peter's church open again.

Determined to be supportive now, Clair asked, "The church administrator is called the verger, is that right? Was there one at St. Peter's when I went with Grandma and Lizzie?"

"There was, but he died. Then the congregation shrank, and everything fell apart. A verger arranges baptisms, weddings, and funerals, coordinates the choir and bell ringing–things, like that. At present, three parishes are covered by one minister, the Reverend, Dr. Tim Fell, and it's just too much for one person. Obviously, I'll be around to see you guys, and train a couple of volunteers to take over the office, if you … if we…"

She stopped, hating the feeling of 'leaving a sinking ship.'

Clair jumped up to give her a hug. "I know you'll leave it all in order, and many congratulations on your new role. I know how much this means to you, and it would be great to have St. Peter's open again. The Reverend Tim doesn't know yet how lucky he is. We're going to miss you terribly, but you'll still be nearby."

Patricia's lovely smile glowed. "Thank you. You told me once that your faith in God died with your family, but I hope you know how many people are praying for you."

There was a knock on the door and Robert stuck his head around.

"Sophie wanted to come back in, so I've put her in the office. Could I see you for a moment, Clair, when you're free?"

Patricia gathered her things. "I need to get on with organizing refreshments, see you later."

Robert came in and dropped into a chair rubbing

big hands across his eyes. He was as tired as everyone else. "I'll come straight to the point. My wife has asked me to stay longer over Christmas, to talk about getting back together. The boys are both working now, but one is still living at home. Will you need me here?"

Clair thought back to the day Robert arrived with Winston. He went back to the city regularly to see his family, but had never mentioned moving back.

"Do you need me?" Robert repeated. "I'll stay, if you want."

"No," Clair was certain. "Of course not. I'm sorry, I was just thinking things through. All the ponies go out during the day. I can manage, with Granddad and obviously look after Winston for you. It sounds important that you go."

Who knew what would happen on January 3rd? Maybe this was his chance to reunite his family? They could sort things out for Winston later.

Clair and Robert walked back from the training room together.

In the horse barn, David was grooming Winston. He'd be riding Rebel in the Nativity pageant, but, like Robert, his closest bond was with the giant grey. He was now on Winston's regular grooming schedule and liked to talk with him.

He smiled as Robert came into the stall to quickly

pick out Winston's hooves for him. "Thanks, I think I'll always be too unsteady to lift these great big feet."

Winston looked around to see who was disturbing his peace and carried on munching hay as Robert followed Clair to the arena.

* * *

David was thinking about the email he'd received on his phone earlier. The CO's admin had set up an interview for a consultant position. Based in London, it would involve Regimental Procurement, working at Army bases all over the world.

The next few days would be his last at the Stables, and David was feeling strange about saying goodbye. All his gear was packed and a company had deep cleaned his apartment. His mother and stepfather were coming to London for the West End shows, and he and Cilla were booked to spend the few days of Christmas with them.

Goodbye to Clair. He was with her every day at rehearsals. He brushed Winston's mane and leaned to softly murmur into the warm neck, "I'm going to miss her. Should I ask Clair to the Regimental Dinner?"

No. It was probably not a good idea. He'd told Cilla

he wasn't going, and perhaps Jack had already asked her to go with him? Clair would be embarrassed, and Jack was needed to sign off that final piece of paper.

He heard Clair's voice in the horse barn and then she was leaning on the half-door, watching him as he brushed Winston's silky tail.

"Doesn't it annoy Cilla that you come to us every day? She must expect you to support her."

David continued brushing. "It's complicated. But Cilla's not the only one who'll be bidding against you, is she?"

Clair picked gloomily at slivers of wood on the door post. "True, but you've become a friend. Everyone says you'll take her side at the auction."

"I'm not taking sides and I won't be in Summerfield by then."

Clair turned and was gone again. David put the grooming tools away.

He stroked Winston's nose and gave him a tiny sweet apple from his jacket pocket. "Good fella, I'm off to the arena now, to watch Nick's first driving lesson. I'm going to miss seeing you as well."

* * *

David had run his idea about Nick and the pony cart past Robert after the soccer evening.

"Why didn't we think of that before? Youngsters could learn in the indoor arena, where Bonnie can't run away with them. Let's go and look at that saddle."

After experimentation, they'd found a way to secure Nick's customized saddle to one side of the driver's bench.

In the arena, Robert was using the hoist to load Nick into the pony cart. Steph was there to strap him in and there were 'high fives' all around.

Ted climbed laboriously into the driving seat and took the reins. "I'm going to need that hoist if we do this too often. You'll have a turn driving in a few minutes, Nick, but first we'll practice the commands. You repeat everything after me, so she'll get used to your voice as well as mine. Walk on, Bonnie."

They set off around the arena, to applause from everyone watching.

* * *

In the training room, Clair heard them clapping as she waited to give feedback to the shepherds after their dress rehearsal. The Nativity Ride was the biggest event she'd ever produced. There were no auditions and in case it was the last, Clair had said that anyone who wanted to be in it, could be! But the shepherds had not brought their costumes to the rehearsal, they came in at the wrong time, and there were tantrums.

"Before you go home, I need you to listen."

She put her 'evil eye' on the noisy group and waited for silence. "Thank you. Everyone's doing a great job, and dress rehearsals are always messy. The glitches will be sorted out by the performance, but the next rehearsal is in the arena, with all performers, horses, lights, and sound. We need to not repeat the mistakes from today. Okay, I'll see you all tomorrow."

* * *

All the volunteers had gone for the day. Ted went into the cottage with Jossie to watch TV, and Robert set off in a minivan to take some students home after the rehearsal.

Clair helped Steph put head collars on all the ponies. "I need some fresh air after all that creative tension! Can you drive the Jeep down with the hay, and I'll follow with the ponies?"

She used the mounting block to hop bareback

onto Bella, who often enjoyed being out with the ponies. With three on leading ropes to either side, Clair followed Steph along the track.

Bella's body was warm beneath her and the woods were silent, with no human voices to disturb the peacefulness. It had been a busy day, and the ponies were tired too. There was no frost tonight, so they could have one more night of freedom before the performance. Everyone would have a rest over the holiday.

Clair negotiated the seven through the top gate and started down the dark track. Moving in the headlights of the Jeep, Steph transferred hay to the rack. Behind her, silhouetted against the far lights of Oxford, two huge diggers stood silent in the mud. Arms locked into the air, they looked like dinosaurs. Happily, since the standoff with Quentin, work had stopped on the boggy meadow.

Clair slid off Bella and Steph helped unclip all the lead ropes. Led by Tosca, the ponies galloped around the field. A few mad minutes and they stopped to pull hay from the rack. All except Bonnie, who, as usual, went straight over to the fence, reaching through to pull at long stems of grass.

Steph and Clair were climbing wearily into the Jeep when they heard a sharp crack. Looking around,

they watched in horror as the fence collapsed with
a splintering sound and Bonnie disappeared.

Chapter 18

Before he left each day, David had become accustomed to saying goodnight to Clair and Steph. By the time he'd cleaned Rebel's tack and put it away, he found the pony stalls empty. Steph had mentioned that the ponies were having one more night in the fields. He'd head home to the Manor House and see them tomorrow.

He was crossing the parking lot to his Jag, thinking about the challenges of riding Rebel when he noticed the headlights of a vehicle. It was bouncing at high speed along the track from St. Peter's.

Steph tore into the parking lot in the Jeep, skidded to a halt, and ran toward the office. "Bonnie's gone through the fence. She's stuck in a ditch and Clair needs help. There's no mobile reception down there, I'm calling the Fire Brigade on the landline."

David reached into the car to grab his second cane. The Jag would be useless in the muddy lane, and if he fell, he would be too.

He hurried after Steph and grabbed keys from the board. "I'll take the tractor."

Chugging past the dark church, the small headlight of the tractor showed the potholes, and curious ponies came to meet him in the field. He carefully skirted the worst of the mud and reached a splintered gap in the fence. All was in deep shadow below the rim of the bank. He held onto the tractor and peered over.

The light behind him cast a huge shadow and Bonnie showed the whites of her eyes, as she plunged madly in a deep ditch.

"Whoa!" Clair hung onto the pony's head collar and he heard the relief in her voice. "David! Thank goodness you hadn't gone! Robert went to Oxford and won't be back for hours. We've got to get Bonnie out of here quickly."

Clair was in the water with the pony, the mud over her gumboots.

He cursed his leg for not being able to climb down to help her. "Are either of you hurt?"

"I'm not, and there's no blood on Bonnie. I think she's just in shock. The sides of the ditch are too steep for us to climb out and the water's freezing. I hope the Fire Brigade get here soon."

Clair stroked the pony's quivering muzzle. But when Bonnie stopped struggling, they both sank deeper into the mud.

Lit by the tractor headlight, David looked at the crisscross of trenches. A monster digger was parked dangerously near them, its crane arm locked up in the air. "This looks like something out of World War I." He turned at the sound of the Jeep returning. "Steph's here. I'll go back to the Stables and call Jack. He might be able to help."

Steph brought the Jeep as close to the fence as she could and left the headlights on to shine her path. David met her halfway with her arms full of horse blankets and gave her a ride back to the fence.

"Ted's waiting for the vet and the Fire Brigade are coming from Woodstock."

"They'll need some sort of strapping to put around Bonnie, to help them to pull her out. Any ideas?"

Steph thought for a moment. "Yes! Her harness for the pony cart is hanging next to the webbing girths. If you brought it and the girths as well, we could strap everything tightly around her."

David left them. Near St. Peter's he got a mobile signal and called Jack. He'd managed to hitch the trailer to the tractor when a massive, red fire truck roared into the yard. Six firefighters climbed out wearing hazard suits and yellow helmets.

"Thanks for getting here so quickly. They've been in the ditch for almost thirty minutes, and the pony's showing signs of hypothermia."

Jack drove in as David pointed out the track past St. Peter's.

"We're Army officers and might be able to help. We'll load some stuff onto the trailer and follow you down."

David and Jack watched as the fire engine disappeared, the big headlights flashing this way and that as it hit bumps. "The track's very slippery and that big truck might not get down there. They may have the equipment to get Bonnie out, but if not, we could try…"

David outlined his idea and they loaded things onto the trailer.

Ted came out of the cottage, looking anxious. "How are they?"

"Luckily, there's no wind chill, but the water's ice-cold in that ditch."

"Tell Clair I'll bring the vet as soon as he arrives."

David and Jack found the fire truck stuck halfway down the muddy field. It had slid sideways toward the wood and was now anchored with four corner braces. But the powerful headlights illuminated everything.

David saw that Steph had caught Bella and the ponies, tying them to the hay rack out of the way. He and Jack chugged over to the gap in the fence.

Clair and Steph had horse blankets around their shoulders but looked pinched with cold.

"Hang in there," David called down to them. "Ted says the vet's coming and the firemen will soon have you out of there."

Bonnie had two extra blankets around her but was dull-eyed and not reacting to firemen shouting instructions and putting planks across muddy trenches.

Jack passed the cart harness and webbing girths to Clair and she roused herself. "Come on Steph, let's slide the harness over the top of the blankets and I'll put this long strap between her front legs."

Steph's hands were frozen, and she fumbled.

"Jack, can you help get that other strap around Bonnie's hindquarters? Okay, let's buckle them all together."

David was watching with the Fire Chief and now he turned to him. "I have a prosthetic leg and can't help down there, but Jack and I have both done survival training in mud. To get a man out, we build a scaffold for leverage. As I see it, the pony must be lifted straight up into the air and out of the mud. If we pull sideways, her legs will break."

The Chief nodded and David pointed up to the metal arm of the digger. "We don't have time to build a scaffold, but I noticed that. It's strong and secure and we brought the big pulley wheel from the hay barn. If your guys could lash it to the top of the digger arm and run a rope around it, we could use the tractor to pull back and lift the pony out."

The Fire Chief immediately called his men and they went into action. Illuminated by the headlights, a fireman climbed the digger and secured the wheel to the top of the arm. He passed a strong nylon rope around it. One end was secured to the harness behind the pony's shoulders and run underneath the girths around her hindquarters.

A fireman unhitched the trailer as Jack ran with the other end of the rope and tied it to the tow bar. David revved the tractor engine. He backed slowly until the rope pulled taut.

"Good to go!"

All the firemen and Jack lined up on the planks to support the pony as she came out. The Chief called, "On the count of three…one, two, three!"

David tightened the rope, and everybody bent down with their arms out. But nothing happened.

Then Clair started jumping up and down, splashing water into the pony's face.

Steph smacked the blanket on her hindquarters and shouted, "Come ON, Bonnie…make an effort!"

The pony jerked awake from her cold trance and thrashed wildly in the water.

The Fire Chief shouted again, "One…two… three!"

David accelerated slowly, the others controlled the rope through the pulley wheel, and, with a horrible slurping sound, Bonnie came free.

She swung in the air, snorting and dripping liquid mud. David brought the tractor slowly back and she was guided to rest with her feet on the planks.

"Hold it there for a minute, guys," David kept the rope taut, to support Bonnie's body weight.

Clair climbed stiffly from the ditch, reaching back to pull Steph out after her. They were dripping with muddy water and could barely walk. But Bonnie was alive and out of the ditch.

Slowly, they brought her onto dry land, just as Ted arrived in the vet's Land Rover. He brought old sheepskin coats for Clair and Steph, plus a bundle of empty cloth feed sacks.

The vet examined Bonnie and gave her an injection as Clair began to strip off her wet blankets. With Ted's guidance, everyone grabbed a feed sack and began to rub Bonnie down. There was laughter as they were soon warm and then the pony suddenly shook out her coat.

"She's going to be okay!"

They all cheered, and a thick, dry horse blanket was strapped around Bonnie.

Clair walked slowly up the track with her and the vet as Steph collected Bella and the ponies on their lead ropes. "So much for a fun last night of freedom, eh, guys? Jack, could you bring the Jeep? Ted's bringing the vet's Land Rover."

He nodded and they both followed her up the hill.

The fireman climbed up again and dismantled the pulley. They loaded their planks and put all the Stables equipment back into the trailer, talking about the rescue.

With some skillful driving, they reversed the big fire truck out of the field. Last to leave, David chugged the tractor back up the track and through the gate, then climbed carefully down to lock it. Looking back, only the splintered gap in the fence indicated any drama played out there that night.

* * *

Ted beckoned to the Fire officers, "Come in, guys, the water's hot for coffee."

The Fire Chief thanked him. "We need to get the truck back to Woodstock, Ted. We'll shower and eat there. Good night, all."

The truck roared up the lane and then Ted began to shake with reaction and anger. "I lost my old horse, Russ, last year. I don't ever want to see a vet euthanize an animal again for as long as I live. We almost lost Bonnie and I'll find that Kidd fella tomorrow, and give him a piece of my mind."

Jack was leaving. "I'm heading home but give me a call tomorrow, and I'll go with you. Gary Kidd can be a nasty piece of work."

David gave him a man-hug, "Thanks for coming so quickly."

"We were lucky," Jack spoke quietly. "Another ten minutes and it would have been a different story. See you tomorrow."

Back in the cottage, David could see Ted was feeling old and shaky. He made him sit by the stove with Jossie.

"I'm the cleanest, so I'll make the coffee."

He made hot beverages and talked reassuringly but was anxious to find Clair. He looked up hopefully when the front door opened and was astonished when Steph came in and threw her arms around him.

"You're a genius, David Brown. It was a great idea to use the pulley and the crane!"

He handed her a mug of coffee with lots of cream and sugar in it, the way she liked. "Thank goodness, it worked. Is Clair coming?"

"She's still with the vet. He says Bonnie should be okay, and he's coming back early tomorrow." Steph drank the coffee quickly. "Thanks! I'm heading home to have a long, hot shower."

Steph went to kiss Ted, then she came back and leaned close to David. "I know it's supposed to be top secret, but I've guessed that Nick's anonymous buddy is you… and I can't thank you enough."

Steph looked very young and her eyes were full of tears. As his answer, David hugged her, but he needed to find Clair. How was she doing?

* * *

Clair was leaning wearily against Bonnie's stall, Ted's old sheepskin coat still buttoned over her muddy clothes. She was watching the pony eat a warm mash.

David knew Clair preferred hot peppermint tea in the evening, so he'd brought a big mug for her.

192

He wrapped her cold hands around the mug and held them there with his own.

"Drink up, then you must take off those wet things."

"I can't leave her."

David put his arm gently around her and supported her hand to sip the tea.

Clair relaxed and leaned against him as they watched Bonnie. "Thank you."

"You're welcome." He gently brushed some dried mud from her face "She's safe now."

"Doing her favorite thing–which is eating ..."

"...like a horse?"

Clair smiled wanly. "I was going to say, 'as if it were her last meal.' But that's scary, because it easily could have been. Exmoors are a hardy breed, but she could have died down there."

Bonnie licked noisily around the bottom of the feed bucket, searching for stray grains. Then she lay down, grunting and stiff, but sleepy from the injection and comfortable in the deep straw.

Her eyes closed and Clair switched off the lights, leaving only the one by the door to the arena. She'd revived a little with the hot tea, so David turned her to look through the doorway. "What?"

"There..."

He pointed to the big mirrors fixed along the

wall. Riders used them to check their posture and the movements of their horse.

Clair started to giggle. "Oh, dear, you are so clean! And I am so unbelievably muddy!"

She began to rock with silent laughter. Breathless and hiccupping, she leaned into David. Holding her in the circle of his arms and looking down into soft brown eyes, caressing her lips with his was as natural as breathing. Then they kissed as if they could never stop.

"In days of old, I'd have swept you into my arms and carried you home. Since I can't do that, hold onto that wall and we'll manage together."

David leaned on his cane and tucked her other arm through his. They walked slowly across the yard, guided by the light from the porch. The minivan was parked back in its bay and they heard Robert's deep voice inside the cottage, speaking with Ted.

"Maybe Robert could keep an eye on Bonnie tonight? You've had a shock. You need food, a long soak in a hot bath, and some sleep." David smiled cheekily at her. "Would you like me to come and help you in the tub?"

Clair grinned back in a tired way. "Thanks, I'll manage."

"If you promise to do those things, then I'll go home now,"

"I promise. Good night…and thank you again."

David transferred Clair's hand to the door, and she leaned in to give him a gentle hug. It was not passionate this time but had all the gratitude of a dear friend. As she drew away, David saw the love in her eyes.

"It's the Regimental Dinner on Saturday night. I know it's short notice, but might you be free to go with me?"

Chapter 19

Early on Saturday evening, Clair watched a long, white limo draw up outside Stables Cottage.

David climbed from the back and by the light in the porch she could see he was clean shaven, his dark hair newly cut. He wore Regimental evening dress in all black, with an embroidered bar of medals over his left top pocket. Were military uniforms designed to make all men look handsome? Or was it just this particular man?

David negotiated the path with one black cane and Clair opened the door. She had her best black coat over the long, silver-grey gown from Lizzie's wedding and the night wind ruffled her hair.

He smiled. "Hi! You've had your hair cut and it looks great!"

At the beauty salon that morning, Clair's hair had

been highlighted ash-blond and cut into the same pixie style she had in Edinburgh.

"Thank you." She smiled back at him. "Granddad said he thought something was different but wasn't quite sure what it was. He wished us a happy evening anyway." Clair pulled the door shut and there came a long howl of misery from the kitchen. "Granddad's having a Christmas meal at Jim's. Jossie can't go with him because he chases Jim's cats."

David offered his hand for her to climb into the warm interior of the limo. Clair said good evening to the driver and slid out of her coat. David hung it on a hook and bent to retrieve the silver-grey wrap that had fallen from her shoulders. It was the same shade as the dress, which shimmered like moonlight on water.

Clair had sent Lizzie a picture from her phone but did not intend to tell David that this was her bridesmaid's dress. It brought back such happy memories that she was glad of the opportunity to wear it again.

David fastened her seatbelt and then his own. "I'm not drinking alcohol and would have driven you in the Jag, but I expect we'll both be tired coming home."

The driver carefully reversed the long vehicle around the horse trailer, and Clair savored the luxurious moment. Robert was on duty and she was going to a Regimental dinner with David! Nerves tingled under her ribs. Would she fit in okay? Or would the women all be like Cilla's horsey crowd?

Clair's starry pendant earrings matched the delicate necklace in the neckline of the dress and caught the light as she moved.

David leaned forward to look at them. "They're beautiful."

"Yes, and of course, in my line of work, I wear diamonds all the time." They both giggled. The limo had left the country lanes and they were on the road to Oxford. "Patricia covered for me while I was at the beauty salon. When I got back, she'd been home to fetch the necklace and earrings. Wasn't that kind?"

David watched her with a half-smile on his face. "It was kind, and the earrings look spectacular with your new hairstyle."

Did he think her unsophisticated? Oh, who cared about sophistication! Clair wiggled her right hand at him, showing off the matt silver fingernails that matched her dress. "I feel guilty saying it, but these hands did nothing for ponies all day."

He took her hand and Clair thrilled at his touch. "You deserve a break. How's Bonnie doing?"

They both leaned back comfortably as the limo sped along in the darkness.

"Almost back to normal, thank goodness! But no more about the Stables or ponies tonight. Tell me about this special uniform and your medal ribbons."

"On Ladies' Night we wear this formal outfit from the history of our Regiment. It honors the wonderful women who support us."

He explained the campaign for each medal ribbon as the limo purred into central Oxford.

Clair's voice bubbled with happiness. "It's fascinating history. I'm delighted to be attending, but I've never been to a function like this and wondered about etiquette."

"There's nothing to worry about. Jack's meeting us there with his partner, so we'll have two friends straight off and you'll meet lots more. We have drinks, then dinner, speeches, and dancing. I can't dance with this leg, so all the single guys will be lining up to dance with you."

Clair was reassured, but David was obviously checking things in his mind. "Okay, I just thought of something. The speeches can go on for two hours, and you can't leave the table in that time."

"Ah, I've been in that kind of situation before! Go easy on the liquids?"

David chortled. "You've got it! Every time your glass is half empty, it must be refilled."

"...so, a delicate hand with silver fingernails will be placed over my glass when someone tries to do that."

The limo drew up in front of the Grand Hotel. A glass atrium glittered white and gold with Christmas decorations and men in the same military evening dress as David ascended the escalator. Their partners wore long dresses in a hundred beautiful shades and patterns.

David was still holding her hand when their turn came to step onto the moving staircase. "Watch out for your heels here, Miss Williams!"

"And prosthetics, Captain Brown!"

They stepped together over the converging metal teeth at the top. As her dress swirled, David glimpsed a tiny blue butterfly tattoo on Clair's ankle.

The Ballroom was already packed with couples and alive with the music of a ragtime band.

"There's Jack!"

Through the military uniforms and gorgeous gowns, Jack came smiling to meet them. Following him, in a sweeping, low-cut, poppy-red dress was Kate McIntyre. Her brown hair was piled high into an elegant topknot and her eyes were fixed on David.

She gave him a long hug before she turned to Clair. "Hi. Jack says this is your first time at a Regimental event. The guys will find the champagne while we visit the powder room."

She smiled at David. "We'll be back in a few minutes."

Clair followed her. Was Kate angry that she was with David? Would tension ruin the evening?

They waited in line for the powder room and her pleasure in the evening deflated. Women ahead of them checked hair and makeup in the mirrors and Clair thought she'd better start a conversation. "This is an amazing venue."

Kate smiled and turned to her. "It is, and we're so glad you could come with David. He's turned down all invitations since his return from Afghanistan and it's great that he's here tonight. You know that he and I have been friends for a while?"

Clair nodded, relieved that Kate was being so open. "I thought you and David might get together in the UK?"

"To tell you the truth, I hoped that we might. But now I accept that we were never together in the romantic sense. If we were going to make it as a couple, it would have happened in Afghanistan. But I last saw David in the hospital and wanted to check if anything had changed. It hadn't. We're the same good friends and now I see the way he looks at you …"

Clair was astonished. How did David look at her? But the line was moving, and Kate continued cheerfully. "Jack is fun and I'm about to go through a big transition to civilian life."

"Can you have Hannibal back?"

Kate shook her head. "Sadly, no. I don't know what I'll be doing nor where I'll be living; but I've been to see him in the new kennels with Anthony and he's doing well.

They returned to the ballroom for champagne and all touched their glasses together. "Cheers!"

Jack smiled at Clair. "Not so muddy here then?"

She grinned back "It's good that we clean up so nicely!"

A uniformed trumpeter now played a fanfare and the Senior Officers led their partners into the Banqueting Suite.

David offered his arm and as Clair took it, she felt his slight tremor. Was he nervous? In pain? It was his first regimental event since the incident. She had been the one shaking after the rescue of Bonnie. But, like that night, David had his cane in his other hand, and together, they were solid.

* * *

The Banqueting Suite of the hotel was painted in a delicate Wedgwood blue, and the long tables sparkled with glass and silverware.

A waiter in military uniform held the chair out for Clair to sit down, and beside her name card was an exquisite box of chocolates. She'd keep those for Patricia. Her diamonds were in good company tonight! Once all the ladies were seated, the officers sat down.

There were several wheelchairs and David leaned close to whisper, "That could be me. Thanks for all your help in beating the vertigo."

The Chaplain stood to say Regimental Grace and an exquisite, five-course dinner was served. Each course had carefully matched wines and Clair sipped her one small glass as they chatted with Jack and Kate.

David introduced her to the officer on her left and his wife. He was a keen polo player and dessert passed pleasantly in animated discussion about polo. Then the Master of Ceremonies introduced the Colonel-in-Chief. A short speech of welcome, and Clair stood with everyone to drink the 'Loyal Toasts.'

"Her Majesty, The Queen." (A sip of wine.)

"The Regiment." (Another sip. All the women sat down.)

The officers stood to attention and Clair's neck prickled with the intensity of David's eye contact. "The Ladies of the Regiment."

But she was not a 'Lady of the Regiment.'

Clair suddenly understood the weight of history and tradition in the room. She'd thought it was a jolly night out, but they were celebrating a culture to which she could never belong. A magical attraction to David was one thing, but she was against violence in any form. What was she doing, dreaming of being with him?

The Regiment was part of David and he wanted to go back to his comrades-in-arms. Whatever happened at the auction, Clair knew now that she could not follow him. She had a life and passions of her own.

And, oh dear, the speeches were tedious! There seemed to be a Regimental language, totally foreign to her and punctuated with guffaws of male laughter. Clair kept an 'interested' look on her face, but behind the facade, her mind wandered further away with each tiny sip of wine.

At last it was over. Clair joined Kate and all the other women heading for the Powder Rooms.

Once inside, a great wave of female voices and laughter washed over her. "Honestly, I didn't think

I could listen to that old bore for one more minute! Wasn't that the same speech as last year?"

Kate covered her mouth in a yawn. "The worst is over, and the dancing is fun. You'll be glad for those sensible heels."

She giggled and indicated two women already comparing sore feet in spiky-heeled evening sandals. They rejoined David and Jack in the Ballroom, where small tables set around the walls were filling up with groups of friends. Colors reflected from a rotating glitter ball across the big dance floor, and a top DJ was winding up the disco.

David held out his hand, to bring her next to him and Jack asked Kate to dance. Clair watched them moving through rainbows on the polished surface. "Several friends have asked if you'd care to dance."

"I'm happy to stay here, if you like. I can dance anytime."

"There are people here tonight that I haven't seen in years. It will be boring for you, but if you're dancing, they'll stop by for a chat."

A good-looking officer with blond hair approached and smiled at Clair. "May I introduce Rory? They're playing a great song and I can see your feet twitching."

Clair enjoyed dancing to several tracks with

Rory but then explained that she wanted to return to their table.

As they approached, an older man with white hair and two rows of medals was just sitting down with David. "That's our Commanding Officer. Dance a bit longer?"

Clair nodded. She watched David from the corner of her eye and could see he was held in high respect. It had been a good experience to come with David, but now she felt tired and a bit sad. It was 2:00 a.m. and she wanted to go home.

The senior officer was gone and back at the table Clair rested a hand on David's arm. "I've had a great time, but Kate says the drinking and dancing go on till dawn. We have final rehearsals on Monday; would it be against etiquette to leave now?"

With coats on, they exited through revolving doors into the shock of a freezing early morning. But the luxury of the limo awaited.

The driver played soft music on the stereo as the car purred toward Summerfield. Clair realized that David was relieved she'd suggested going home. She stretched her seatbelt to the maximum and nestled against his shoulder. With his arm around her, her eyes closed, and she drifted in the warmth. They were quiet and comfortable until the limo drew up at Stables Cottage.

The moonlight was bright white across May's garden and Jossie barked as David walked Clair to the door.

"Thank you so much for taking me."

Clair hesitated, thinking of the kiss that might end such an evening. But David did not move, and no fire flashed between them.

"I enjoyed being with you very much. Could we go for a walk tomorrow afternoon, Clair? There's so much I want to tell you."

Chapter 20

David was sitting on the bottom stair in the Manor House, lacing up the walking boot that matched his titanium leg. He was thinking about Clair. He saw her again in his mind's eye, tall and slender, in an elegant gown that shimmered like water. Other women he knew were so blasé about diamonds, and he smiled, remembering her freshness and laughter.

Cilla's bedroom door slammed, and she came down the staircase behind him. "What's going on, David? You told me you weren't going to the Regimental dinner, but then you went–with Clair Williams, of all people! Zara just called to tell me."

She watched him like a snake, and he was tired of her interference.

"I'm packing today and moving back to my London apartment at the end of the week."

* * *

At Stables Cottage, he watched Clair wrap a big, striped muffler around her neck and tuck the ends into a thick, navy jacket. Each finger of her gloves was a different color.

"These are an early Christmas present from Lizzie. I haven't even had time to send Christmas cards this year, but I know she'll understand. She and Harry are in Oxford after Christmas, so I'll take them out to dinner then."

Clair was talking very fast, being bright and cheerful. Jossie bounced up to David, then dashed off along his favorite path into Potlatch Wood. Then Clair was silent but walking so fast he soon needed to stop and rest. She stopped and came back. "Sorry."

"It's fine. I was enjoying being with a woman who doesn't talk at me all the time."

"I was trying to be mysterious, as opposed to normal and boring."

David looked at her for moment, then grinned. "I like the normal bit, and you're never boring."

Then they laughed. Jossie had picked up a stick four times as long as his body and was trying to push it between two trees. He threw his whole weight behind it, growling between clenched teeth and refusing to give up. Clair offered him a treat from her pocket and grabbed the stick when he opened his mouth to take it. He swallowed the treat and tried to jump for the stick again, but she held it in the air.

"No, Jossie. Leave it!"

Luckily, he picked up the scent of a rabbit and was soon off again, weaving through the undergrowth.

David walked on as Clair slashed at some nettles with the stick, then threw it away and caught up.

"Yesterday was sad for Granddad and me so I wanted to thank you again, especially, for last night. It was the anniversary of when my parents and Owen were killed."

David stopped and looked at her in shock. "I'm so sorry. Ted showed me the gravestone, but I didn't register the dates."

"It's okay. We went to St. Peter's, took flowers, and talked of the good times. There's only a certain amount of that kind of remembering that anyone can take. It was wonderful to dress up in the evening and go out."

"Losing them must have been a terrible blow."

Clair stuffed her hands into the pockets of her jacket and kicked leaves with her gumboots. "I was totally numb for months, maybe years. I finally put my feelings into a box and shut the lid. It was my grandparents and horses that helped me cope."

They reached a massive pile of dry leaves, blown like a snow drift, into the shelter of a fallen tree. "My leg's sore after yesterday, could we sit down for a bit?"

"Of course, sorry, I was carried away by my thoughts."

David lowered himself into the leaves, his back against the tree trunk and Clair came to sit next to him. "But you lost your mum too, when you were young, didn't you?"

"Yes, but not tragically. She was still in the world, just not with Cilla and me. I think you know Anthony is Cilla's and my half-brother? Dad's first wife, Anthony's mum passed away and he married Nancy, our mum, who is American. Their marriage was in trouble by the time I was four years old."

Clair listened, leaning her head back against the tree. "What happened?"

"Dad's always been a wealthy playboy and he continued to have affairs. He fought for custody in the divorce court, to keep Cilla and me in this country. He always needs to win, and he did. But after that we had a succession of nannies and then got sent to boarding school."

"How was that for you? We only saw you back in Summerfield for the occasional vacation."

"Cilla hated her school, but I actually enjoyed mine. I thrived on endless sport and being an Army cadet. We spent summer vacations in California, with Mum and Scott, her second husband. Sometimes we flew out to be with Dad on the yacht."

Clair smiled. "Doesn't sound too bad! I love England, but never had the chance to go overseas. There was never enough money, but I loved coming to Ted and May in school vacations."

She picked up a leaf skeleton and studied it. "On the day of the accident, I'd been here a week. They were due to join us, but a vehicle broke down in the fast lane of the motorway. Four cars ploughed into it, there was a big pile-up. Six people were killed, my family among them."

Clair was quiet, twizzling the leaf back and forth. "Do the bad memories ever go away? I try to move on, but it's all still there in the back of my mind."

David took the hand that wasn't holding the leaf. "I think it gets easier, but never goes away completely. Whatever doesn't kill you makes you stronger, and all that. I'm still having counseling about Afghanistan. They tell me the memories don't fade if you keep pushing them down. Did you ever see a counselor?"

Clair shook her head. "Granddad's generation went through war and death, just expected to deal with it. Counseling wasn't something that ever occurred to them. Horses and dogs are my counselors, and my family. I know you understand that. You had military ancestors and your family is the Army."

"I do understand, and it's what I wanted to talk to you about. A senior officer spoke with me last night and wants me to take an exciting job with him."

Clair looked down at their linked hands. "Then you'll be back with your buddies."

"I've missed the companionship and there would be a lot of interesting travel."

There was an awkward silence. "It's probably better I'm gone, anyway. I hope you win the lease, but with Cilla bidding, it makes life difficult."

Clair let go of David's hand, lay back in the leaves and gazed at the sky between bare branches. High above them was a huge bunch of mistletoe.

With a sigh, she slowly rolled over toward David and braced herself on her elbows, looking into his eyes. "I knew you were going to say something like that. I understand you want to be 'just friends,' but I want to kiss you, just for goodbye." She smiled sadly and pointed up at the mistletoe.

David was motionless, then he reached for

her. Clair's eyes closed and she responded to the breathtaking electricity that ran between them. Kissing her lips and eyelids in an entirely beautiful moment, David murmured her name.

"Mmmm … don't stop."

"We must, it's not fair to either of us."

Clair put a finger on his lips, "I understand Summerfield is a temporary stopover for you. If you asked Kyle, you'd find I don't have casual flings anyway."

They had entirely forgotten Jossie. At that moment there was a mad scuffling in the leaves and a large black Labrador hurdled over the tree trunk, landing right on top of them. Jossie followed, barking with excitement as a large wet pink tongue covered Clair's face with licks.

She gasped and rolled away from David. "Eeerrgh, Jester! Get off!"

Jossie followed Jester chasing through the leaves and David was laughing fit to bust. Clair managed to stand up and was brushing leaves from her jeans when Kyle strolled down the path.

"Sleeping with the enemy now, are we?"

Clair turned on him, "I'm wide awake, thank you. Why do you always turn up and spoil everything?"

Kyle glanced at David then frowned at Clair. "I can walk my dog anywhere I like. When Gary gets the lease, I hope you won't be around any longer, to spoil the woods for me."

He stomped past them and both dogs raced after him.

Clair whistled for Jossie and David reached for his cane. "Can you give me a hand here, please? Since you're the one who pushed me so deep into these leaves!"

She took his hands, leaned backward and hauled him to his feet.

David dusted himself off. "Interesting that Kyle didn't come too close, considering I was already down. He could have tried kicking me."

Clair snorted and put Jossie on his leash. "I shall never speak his name again, it's like invoking an evil genie, but I reckon he learned his lesson last time with you. He probably thought you'd scissor his legs between yours, rip off your prosthetic and club him senseless."

David looked at her admiringly. "Good thinking!"

He steadied his balance and drew her close to him. Clair did not resist but put her arms around his waist and leaned her head against his chest. David smelled of clean skin and a woodsy aftershave. She breathed in deeply, to hold it in her memory.

He felt for her left hand and placed a small round

rock in it. "It's a tiny potlatch. It stuck in my back when Jester jumped us."

Clair closed her fingers around it as Jossie wound his leash around both their legs. She knew David was leaving immediately after the Nativity ride and she looked up at him. "When's your final interview?"

"January 3rd."

Chapter 21

It was nearly dark at 3:00 p.m. for the Nativity Ride at Summerfield Stables. The lights had all been on since morning and the air was scented with pine branches everywhere. Parents and friends would soon arrive, and Clair recognized now what a huge undertaking it had been. Telling the Christmas story with youngsters and horses? Impossible! Yet they were about to do it.

The sandy floor of the arena was raked smooth and volunteers were doing a final check of the seating. There were traditionally no tickets sold for the end-of-year event, but Sid was handing out clean, red buckets.

"This year, we really do need to collect buckets of money."

"Ha-ha!"

Bursts of singing from the kitchen, accompanied the final sound checks by volunteer technicians. Spotlights were on final test in the arena, and helpers were making spiced fruit juice and laying Christmas cookies on trays.

Clair closed the big doors between the horse barn and arena. All the bank presentations were complete. This was the final fundraising event before Sid would tally the final figure. Would it be enough?

She walked through the pony stalls, marveling at the tossing of heads and jingling of bits. The horses and ponies were as excited as the students, and it sounded like the preparations for a medieval tournament. Winston, playing the part of the Angel Gabriel, would be ridden by Maddie. She'd stenciled silver stars on his hindquarters, swathed him in white gauze, and fixed a shining star on his headband. It nodded vigorously as he bent to watch her paint his hooves silver and Clair laughed–nothing ever seemed to phase this horse!

Then she stopped short.

Two Roman soldiers stood under a light at the end of the barn, their helmets under their arms. One was telling the other something and then they both roared with laughter. What did guys talk about that made them laugh like that? She guessed it wasn't women, more likely sports results, or difficulties with computers.

David had no further attacks of vertigo after the gun scare and his lessons were complete. Today he'd ride Rebel in the pageant, Jack would sign him off and he'd return to the British Army. Clair loved his face, angular and sharply defined in the light. Both soldiers wore short-sleeved khaki tops and breastplates. Beneath the leather kilts, both had black riding pants. With high-topped Roman sandals on strong legs, David Brown looked every inch a military Commander.

Clair hurried away to check on the shepherds in the training room. These were the boys she worried most about. They were walking, not riding, and Clair came into a noisy game of American football. In long rustic robes, with striped tea towels for headdresses, they were calling passes and chucking toy lambs to one another. When they saw her, they stopped and grinned and Clair grinned back.

"Just a bit quieter, guys. The audience are coming in now."

Ted was the Innkeeper and the first to enter the arena at the start of the pageant. Then the Shepherds would come in at the far end. Ted came to sit with the boys now, and folded his hands, one on top of the other on his cane.

He smiled up at Clair and she bent to kiss his dear face, "Granddad, in that brown homespun robe, you are the most perfect Biblical Innkeeper."

Through the small window overlooking the arena, she could see the portable electric organ on the low stage and the organist warming up the choir. Patricia had organized her group from St. Mary's and Tim, the minister, said he'd gladly be the Narrator. The seating was filling and everywhere was extra bright with spotlights and Christmas decorations of holly and ivy from Potlatch Wood. Everyone knew the arena had no heating, so they were coming in bundled up in warm coats, assorted hats, scarves, and gloves! Friends waved and called to each other as Clair slipped back to the horse barn.

Steph had prepared the Holy Family for their entrance. Mary was seated side-saddle on a quiet jenny donkey and Joseph, played by Jack, led them between the horse stalls. Their place was in front of Winston and Maddie was now mounted. A white satin gown covered the saddle and her legs. Her long, blond hair floated loose like gossamer between the huge silver wings. Through the speakers came the opening notes of the first carol and the arena darkened to blackout.

Voices hushed and the choir sang. "Oh, little town of Bethlehem, how still we see thee lie ..."

Clair did a 'thumbs up' to the waiting performers and whispered, "Good luck everyone; careful riding now!"

The carol ended, and spotlights came up on Ted in front of his inn. There was a smattering of gentle applause. Many in the audience knew and loved Ted Williams. His Inn was constructed of hurdles and bales of straw. Ted had borrowed a piebald goat from a farmer friend and seeing him appear, it set up a piteous bleating from its pen. This raised a laugh and Ted fed it pony nuts from a bucket as the spotlights swung to the Shepherds.

They came from the cold, dark world outside and Clair had told them to have fun in this bit. They pushed and shoved each other, laughing as they walked, then sat down at the far side of the arena from Ted. Their campfire was made of red paper, logs, and flashlights.

The Narrator's voice came softly through the speakers. "And there were shepherds abiding in the fields, keeping watch over their flocks..."

The organ played the opening chords, then choir and audience sang "While Shepherds Watched their Flocks by Night."

From the darkness, Clair studied the faces in the audience as they shared the carol sheets to sing. She knew so many of them and she swallowed hard, acknowledging that this event could be the last.

Tim's voice was clear, "A decree went out from Caesar Augustus, that all must return to be taxed in the town of their birth. Joseph came to Bethlehem with Mary, his wife, who expected their baby very soon."

Two volunteers swung the double doors wide open to the starry night. Joseph and Mary had travelled far and were tired. The choir softly sang, "Little donkey, little donkey, on your weary way." Mary's robes and headdress shimmered soft blue as Joseph led the donkey around the arena to the inn. But it was full, there was no room.

The Innkeeper was obviously a kindly soul and led them to his stable, where a goat was already in residence. He brought them food and put hay in the manger for the donkey.

As the lights dimmed, Tim's voice came softly. "And the time came for Mary's baby to be born."

The spotlights swung to the same big doors again and in came Winston. His ears were forward, his eyes were shining, and his long tail floated out, like Maddie's hair. He looked so pleased with himself that the audience cheered.

Behind him came Clair's most challenged youngsters, the choir of angels. Their ponies were draped in shiny, white fabric, and supervising volunteers wore black pants and tops with black gloves. These students were not strong enough to wait in the cold, so they had been dressed at home and arrived a few minutes earlier. They rode their ponies behind Winston, each little one dressed in white gauze with delicate wings and a halo of tiny lights around their riding helmets. For Clair, watching the wonder on their faces was the true meaning of Christmas.

Winston reached the Shepherds and they cowered in fear, arms up to shield them from the light.

"An angel of the Lord appeared and said, 'Do not be afraid, for I bring you news of great joy. Today, in Bethlehem, is born a Savior, who is Christ the Lord. Go now and you will find the Babe, lying in a manger.'"

The choir began the carol, "Hark the herald angels sing," and the audience joined in.

Angels on ponies progressed slowly around the ring and volunteers carefully grouped them around Mary and the Baby. Joseph, the donkey, Innkeeper and goat stood nearby, and the Shepherds arrived, to reverently lay their lambs beside the manger.

"We three kings of Orient are bearing gifts we travel afar."

Now it was Emily's turn to enter with her

volunteers, mounted on a sparkling-clean, snowy-white Tosca. A long, white gown covered her legs and saddle; a cloud of LED lights flickered all over her. Tonight, Emily was the 'Star of Bethlehem' leading the Kings to find the Christ Child.

Tears welled in Clair's eyes to see the joy on her face. Emily was the same age as Owen when he died. He never experienced anything like this, but Clair was sure that Em would remember tonight for the rest of her life. Her passion burned anew. Even if they lost the lease, she would always work with children like Emily.

Tim's voice was animated now, "Three Kings came from the East and asked, 'Where is the one who has been born King of the Jews? We saw his Star and are come to worship Him.'"

The three students playing the Wise Men were able-bodied and rode their own horses. With golden crowns and robes of crimson, peacock, and emerald, they followed the Star to the stable.

"They saw the Child with Mary, His mother. Opening their treasures, they worshipped Him with gifts of gold, frankincense, and myrrh."

Clair cued the Roman Soldiers. David grinned as he passed her on Rebel. There was a flash of white teeth and dark eyes beneath a helmet.

The lights dimmed on the Stable and flickered

across the arena with the rolling sound of an approaching storm. Then the audience saw ominous shadows at the outer doors. More thunder, and two Roman Soldiers cantered in on big, black horses. The taller of the two had Clair's heart.

They rode arrogantly along beside the seating, and shouted at the audience, "Where are the foreign terrorist spies? We know they came this way. Where are they hiding? And where has a baby been born here tonight?"

Clair had planted students in the audience to mock the soldiers from the darkness. Shaking their fists and shouting threats, Robert and David cantered around the arena, pretending to search for the baby, to kill Him for Herod the King. David was steady in the saddle and Rebel was well under control. Reins in his left hand, sword upraised in his right, no one could tell which of his legs was a prosthetic. The Romans did not find the baby and galloped out through the outer doors.

The main lights came up slowly in the arena and all the spotlights focused on the tableau around the Holy Family. The traditional Bible story ended with everyone singing," Oh, Come All Ye Faithful."

There was applause and lots of cheering.

Clair sighed with relief and handed direction over to Steph. Quietly, she got the volunteers to lead horses, ponies, and students back to the stalls.

The audience stood to applaud and their youngsters waved as Tim Fell spoke into the microphone. "It will be a few minutes before our students return to us for refreshments, but … do you hear what I hear?"

Everyone listened, there was a jingling of sleigh bells through the speakers and to a burst of "Jingle Bells," the big doors opened again.

In trotted Bonnie, dressed as a reindeer, with the pony cart disguised as a sleigh! Robert and Nick were up front, as Santa's Elves and Father Christmas waved from the back of the sleigh. Anthony had been recruited by David and looked very jolly in the Santa costume. Of course, he had his own white beard and shouted, "Ho! Ho! Ho!", inviting the children in the audience into the arena.

Robert jumped down to hold Bonnie's head and parents brought little ones to pat her, while Nick handed out candy canes.

The kitchen helpers now brought out the trestle tables. They served fruit punch and cookies as students gradually returned to their families. All the little angels went home with party bags of cookies and now Clair stepped onto the stage, the spotlights sparkling in her eyes.

"Very well done, everybody!" She led the applause.

"Such enthusiasm and hard work, it was a great performance! I also want to thank the technical team, the kitchen elves, and all our volunteers, without whom Summerfield Stables could not function."

There was more applause and cheering.

"Now, on your way out, we need you to throw HUGE amounts of big bills into the collection buckets! Sid, our financial wizard, will tally the final amount and we can't tell you any figures right now…"

People groaned and Clair grinned. "But I want to assure you, that thanks to your efforts, we have raised a substantial sum! We will definitely be bidding for the lease, on January 3rd."

She struggled to hold her emotions. "Now it's time to celebrate Christmas with our families and friends. Happy Holidays, and safe journey home."

With a repeat of "Jingle Bells," people streamed out of the doors and there were happy discussions of the performance in the horse barn. Tack and finery were taken off and put away. Hay nets went into stalls, water buckets were checked, and there were treats all around for horses and ponies. Lots of pats and praise as the last students and volunteers gathered their things "Goodnight, many thanks, and Happy Holidays!"

David appeared in the doorway of the training room, with a small parcel wrapped in beautiful Christmas paper. It had long, scarlet ribbons and a card.

He held it out to Clair. "Anthony and I are leaving now, to meet up with my mother in London. I've given everyone else their gifts and I chose this for you."

Clair looked down at the gift in her hands and back at David. She had thought of so many ways to say goodbye, but now nothing came to mind. Anthony's voice called, "Are you there, David? We're ready to go."

"On my way."

He was nervous and did not reach out to touch her. "I've written a message in the card; but thanks for everything, Clair. Take care of you and Ted ... Merry Christmas."

Chapter 22

In bed, Clair tossed and turned. She replayed every part of the performance and David's departure, over and over in her mind. She fell into a deep sleep, full of strange dreams and woke at 6:00 a.m. with an explosive sneeze. She was hot and cold with chills.

"You stay there." Ted was firm. "You're tired out. Robert's here for the next three days. He and I can cover everything."

After he left for the Stables, misery washed over Clair and she ached all over. Death had taken Mum, Dad and Owen, then Grandma May. If they lost the auction, she was sure Ted would die. Even though she'd never really had him, David was lost to her too. She'd fallen for a man who was neither physically nor emotionally available.

Clair cried and mopped at her swollen nose with

endless tissues. In between enormous sneezes, she heard the front door open, and Steph called her name.

"Clair, I've brought you some soup. I'll be up there with it in a minute."

Clair sat up and tidied her sheets before Steph appeared in the doorway with a soup bowl and spoon on a tray.

"You look terrible." She placed the tray on Clair's bedside table and then retreated to the door. "I won't come too close. I mustn't catch whatever you've got, because Nick and I are going to my sister's this afternoon."

Clair spooned chicken soup into her mouth and swallowed painfully. "Thanks for the soup. Granddad's specialty is toast." Sadly, she could not taste anything, but it was good of Steph to bring it.

"That's Mum's famous homemade chicken soup, made from Selena's organic chicken, not Kidd's Chunky Chicks! She swears by it when we're sick."

Clair hoped she'd be tactful and not mention David, but no such luck.

"Nick will be with his cousins for the first Christmas in years. David gave him the latest virtual-reality headset, and he can't wait to show it off. He gave Patricia, Robert, and me amazing gift cards! The Sales open on the 26th, and I'm going to buy some new clothes."

Steph waited expectantly as Clair sneezed three gigantic sneezes, one after the other and mopped her nose.

"Sorry, I'm drowning here. David gave Granddad a pair of thermal gloves, like the military guys use in Antarctica and I got some lovely perfume. I can't smell it right now, but it looks nice.

Steph leaned against the doorpost. "He gave the volunteers gift cards too and took Robert to the feed store, to fill the treat bins with apples. He said he'll email me about Nick when he's settled into his new job."

Clair blew gently on the next spoonful of soup. David had obviously said far more to Steph than to her. She didn't even have his email address. Steph glanced at her watch, "Oops, need to go! We'll be back on the 30th and I'll come to see you then. Rest up, get well soon."

★ ★ ★

Robert fed the horses and Ted fed Clair: she ate tea and toast; canned, baked beans in tomato sauce on toast; and boiled eggs with toast.

On the 23rd, the day before Christmas Eve, she

was back on her feet and took over from Robert. "Seriously, I'm fine now and you need to get going. We'll see you at Patricia's for dinner on New Year's Eve."

* * *

Short days and long nights. It was mid-winter, the time of hibernation in the northern hemisphere and the land was asleep.

All the horses and ponies went out in the top fields during the day, wearing their blankets against the cold. Clair brought them in again at 3:00 p.m. and fed them generously. They were warm and comfortable in their stalls as the wind and icy rain battered against the walls of the Stables.

In previous years, she'd used this down time to plan new projects, but there were no students around, the future of the Stables hung in the balance and David was gone forever.

Clair worked hard at being cheerful and watched TV with Ted. But after he was asleep, she prowled the cottage. All was silent, except for the owls in Potlatch Wood and she was angry with herself. There was no communication from David, but what did she expect? In a mad moment, Clair thought about calling his number but managed to control the urge. Jossie followed her anxiously as she picked things up and put them down again, irritated by all the little things that needed fixing.

"He's a soldier, and they often need to go to places they don't want to go. Whatever; he didn't want to stay here with us."

Jim was with his daughter for Christmas, Robert and Patricia were with their families and noisy celebrations at the Potlatch were the last thing Clair needed. She decided to make a special effort for Ted, because it might be their last holiday at Stables Cottage. She studied May's cookbooks and did the grocery shopping. Clair set the table with decorations on Christmas Day and was pleased to serve up her traditional turkey with all the trimmings.

"That looks great, thank you, dear." Ted was pleased. They pulled crackers and wore their colored paper hats to take special treats to all the horses and ponies. Jossie had a delicious Christmas doggie dinner and Clair patted him. "You can go on day after day with a broken heart, if you know how to pretend."

Jossie agreed with everything she said, his eyes glued to the last cocktail sausage in the roasting pan. Thankfully, the days passed, and Robert returned on the morning of New Year's Eve. They all went to Patricia's for a relaxing New Year's Eve meal.

Patricia sold her family home in Oxford when she retired to Summerfield. She'd bought two joined, Victorian cottages behind St. Peter's and was renovating them, in partnership with a builder friend she knew. Patricia opened the front door and greeted them with hugs as Sophie wove around their legs and wagged her tail. "You're my first guests since we completed Number 1, Half-Moon Cottages! Next door, Number 2, is almost finished."

Patricia showed them around, then settled Ted and Robert with beers in front of the log fire. Clair wanted to learn how to make a soufflé so sat up at the breakfast bar with a big glass of red wine.

"Your family must be so impressed! You've done wonders with this cottage."

Patricia popped homemade sausage rolls and vegetarian tartlets into the top oven and folded egg whites with her electric mixer for the soufflé.

"Thank you, they are; and I had a lovely time with them all over Christmas. Okay, the bottom oven's now at the correct temperature and the soufflé goes in for twenty minutes. This is one of Robert's favorite dishes and I made it especially for him. Now, silverware. Everything comes out together when the timer pings, ready to eat immediately."

Clair was thinking of David. "Don't you ever get lonely here? Maybe think about having another partner?"

Patricia opened a drawer to find silverware and napkins. "No. Ron and I married young and we had four children. I never had the chance to go to college. We worked hard to put them through school. They had careers and we had grandkids. Just as we were thinking of fun things to do in our retirement, Ron died. It was a terrible shock."

Clair leaned on the workbench, listening intently, and Patricia smiled at her. "I grieved for him for three years. But then I began to enjoy my own company. There were things I'd always wanted to do, like study for something and have a dog. Ron was allergic to pet hair. Now I have Sophie and it's been fun helping you at the Stables. I can't wait to get started at St. Peter's! There are some lovely men in the world, but I don't see me in another intimate relationship."

The soufflé rose steadily behind the glass door of the oven. "I know it's sensitive for you and Ted, but I wanted you to know that the cottage next door will be ready at the end of January. I need to rent it out to supplement my pension. I hope, with all my heart that you win the auction; but if not, maybe you and Ted might be my first tenants?"

Clair put down her glass, "That's so kind!" Tears were threatening to spill. "I've racked my brains for what to do if we need to move. Granddad will be sad to leave the place he's lived in all his life, but how could we leave Grandma May? Visiting her at St. Peter's is the most important thing in his life."

The timer pinged and Patricia handed her the silverware. "Good. Then the offer is there and hopefully, you won't need to take it up."

"Amen to that."

Robert jumped to his feet as they carried everything to the table. "Look at that, Ted, a perfect cheese soufflé. Thank you, Patricia!"

After the delicious food, they watched the London fireworks on TV and as Big Ben chimed midnight, stood to touch their glasses together.

"Happy New Year!"

Robert echoed all their thoughts, "And success at the auction!"

They drank to that and so ended a happy evening. Half hour later, driving home in the crisp night air, Clair noticed that Ted was coughing.

Chapter 23

Despite his earlier advice to Clair, Ted would not stay in bed. "Stop fussing over me. I'll have a glass or two of whiskey and hot lemon."

But the cough was still harsh and painful on the night before the auction. Early on the morning of the 3rd, Ted looked and sounded much worse. Clair insisted they go to the Health Center in Banbury.

"But you've got the auction; this can wait."

"No, it can't wait," Clair snapped at him. "I should have taken you yesterday, but you are so stubborn. If we go now, I'll still be back in time to bid. We'll never get a doctor to come out here. If you don't behave, I'll call the vet!"

She loaded Ted, well wrapped up, into the Jeep, and drove him to Banbury. The Health Center, as usual, was busy. Without a prior appointment, they needed to take a number in a long line of people waiting to see the doctor. Clair called Sid and told him to bid for them if she was not back. But after all they'd been through, Clair really wanted to be there.

Eventually, Ted was examined and given a prescription for a chest infection. Clair took him for a late breakfast in the coffee shop next door while they waited for the pharmacy to fill the prescription. The line to collect medications was even longer than to see a doctor but at last, they had the prescription filled and headed home.

Clair did not want Ted to see her anxiety, but in the Jeep, she sneaked glances at her watch. They arrived back at 12:40 p.m. The auction was at 1:00 p.m., and the parking lot was full. Clair squeezed the Jeep through a gap between two vehicles and parked it on the grass behind Stables Cottage.

Arm in arm with Ted, she walked to the front door and gave him a kiss on the cheek. "Shall I come in with you, Granddad?"

"No, dear, thank you. I'll take the tablets and go to bed. I'll be thinking of you. Good luck! Come tell me about it later."

* * *

The tiered seating in the arena was packed with people, but Clair saw few familiar faces. Auctions like this were entertainment for farmers and developers. As well as the serious bidders, many came out of interest, to see the property and monitor property prices. Clair had been to a few such auctions herself.

Searching the crowd, she spotted Sid standing where they'd agreed, by the Emergency exit. It was the best place to observe other people and have a clear line to the auctioneer on the stage. Sid's face lit up as Clair pushed her way toward him through the crowd.

"Excuse me, excuse me. Sorry…"

Someone patted her arm as she passed. "Good luck!"

She smiled her thanks and made eye contact with Steph, who was also moving across the arena to Sid. Clair caught baleful stares from Kyle and Gary Kidd, before she and Steph both arrived at Sid's location at the same moment.

Clair hugged them both. "Whew, just in time!"

"How's Ted?"

"He still has that awful cough, but he's got antibiotics, so it should be better soon. The doctor said to bring him back tomorrow morning if they don't kick in. He wished us luck and went back to bed."

"That's good. Patricia and Robert are over there."

Patricia waved and Robert gave a thumbs up sign. A woman in front of them spoke to her neighbor, "Looks like the Bartlett-Browns are here for the kill."

Clair gasped and looked wildly around. Was David there? But no, it was just Cilla, seated in the front row between Anthony and a professional-looking guy with a briefcase.

Steph pointed and laughed. "Is that stuffed with money, do you think? Or is it just his sandwiches?"

She leaned closer and whispered. "Can you tell me now how much we raised?" Clair whispered back, "Keep your face blank when I tell you — we have a million pounds."

Sid had been watching the main door. "Here we go!"

Quentin Ogilvy entered with the auctioneer and they walked to the low stage. Clair remembered the Nativity choir there, but now there was just a table with flyers on it. She'd seen this auctioneer before. He was an older man with receding hair and glasses, wearing a brown suit and blue tie. He tapped on the table with a small wooden hammer.

"Ladies and gentlemen, good afternoon."

It was just past 1:00 p.m. The arena was silent, and all eyes were on him. "Today, we are offering the lease of the Summerfield Stables, a unique property with excellent amenities. The property comprises a considerable acreage of grazing land, stables, barns, and a three-bedroom cottage. The Title remains with the Duke's Estate, but this is a lease of 999 years."

Clair's heart thundered and Steph nudged her. "Breathe."

"The indoor arena," the auctioneer gestured around him, "is the property of the former leaseholders and not included in today's sale. Its purchase can be arranged later, if required."

There was a pause, as he looked down at his paperwork to check his instructions. "Now, would someone like to start at £500,000, for the Lease of the Summerfield Stables?"

No one moved.

Then Cilla raised her hand. Clair's hands were icy.

"£500,000, I have, thank you, Miss Bartlett-Brown. Now, at £600,000, anywhere?"

Sid was experienced from other auctions and they'd talked about following the competition. He whispered to Clair, "It's a high start, but you might as well get in there."

Clair raised her hand. "Thank you, £600,000 is bid by Miss Williams."

No one else came in and the bidding rose rapidly, back and forth between Cilla and Clair.

"£700,000, Miss Bartlett-Brown, thank you … "

"… and £800,000 from Miss Williams."

The room held its collective breath.

"I now have a bid of £900,000, from Miss Bartlett-Brown."

Clair raised her eyebrows at Sid. How could they have arrived at this point so quickly? Gary Kidd had not even made a move, and this was their last shot. Praying Cilla could not go above a million, Clair put up her hand.

"Thank you, I have a bid of one million pounds, from Miss Williams on this side. Do I have 1.1 million offered?"

Cilla turned and spoke sharply to her advisor. Clair saw the faint shake of his head and Quentin Ogilvy smiled briefly at Gary Kidd. There was such blatant collusion between them she wanted to scream.

But the auctioneer was watching Cilla and asked again, "It's against you, Miss Bartlett-Brown, at one million pounds. Would you care to bid?"

Cilla's expression was bitter as she slowly shook her head. The auctioneer acknowledged her withdrawal and Clair breathed again. But there was no cause for celebration.

"The bid now stands at 1 million pounds with Miss Williams. Do I have 1.1 million offered?"

Gary Kidd made a signal and the auctioneer's voice came alive again. "Thank you, I have a bid of 1.1 million from Mr. Kidd."

Clair slumped against the wall and closed her eyes. All their efforts had been for nothing. They had lost the Stables.

A Banbury dairy farmer came in against Gary.

"We have a new bidder. Thank you, Mr. Turner, a bid of 1.2 million, against you, Mr. Kidd."

Clair opened her eyes again and whispered, "Please, if we can't have it, don't let Gary Kidd win."

"A bid of 1.3 million pounds from Mr. Kidd. Against you, Mr. Turner. Do I see 1.4 offered?"

The dairy farmer shook his head and Gary Kidd smirked.

"The bid is 1.3 million pounds. Do I see 1.4 million anywhere in the room?"

The auctioneer scanned the arena.

"Are we all done? If there are no more bids, I am selling the Lease of the Summerfield Stables at 1.3 million pounds. Going once at 1.3 million. Going twice…"

Then a strong male voice rang out from the back. "Two million pounds."

Everyone turned and the auctioneer glanced at

the Land Agent. He immediately looked to Gary Kidd. "We have a new bidder. Your name, sir?"

People moved to one side as David stepped forward.

"David Bartlett-Brown. I have registered my funding online with your office. I bid two million pounds for the Lease of the Summerfield Stables."

"At two million pounds then, a bid from Mr. Bartlett-Brown. It's against you, Mr. Kidd, do I have 2.1 million?"

Gary Kidd's face was a blotchy red. Two million pounds was an outrageous price for an agricultural lease, and he scowled at David. All eyes were on him and he hesitated for a long moment. Then he shook his head.

"At two million pounds then, if I have no other bidders…?"

The silence in the arena hurt her ears.

"… the Lease of the Summerfield Stables is going once at two million pounds … going twice at two million … and going for the third and final time, at two million pounds."

The hammer fell with a resounding crash. "Sold to Mr. David Bartlett-Brown, the Lease of Summerfield Stables, for two million pounds."

Cilla jumped up and squealed with glee. There

was uproar as she pushed through the crowd to her brother and flung her arms around him.

Clair turned blindly out of the Emergency exit and ran.

Chapter 24

David struggled to follow Clair but was held back by Cilla and penned in by the crowd. People thumped him on the back.

"Congratulations!"

Across their heads, he made eye contact with Anthony and pointed in the direction of the auctioneer. His brother nodded but his sister thought he'd bought the Stables for her.

"I had no idea you were going to bid! Why didn't you tell me? Oh, this is marvelous, we can do amazing things with this place."

"I'm sorry," David's face was confused. "We never discussed buying the lease together and when we were in London, I had no intention of even bidding. I bought the lease for Clair."

Cilla froze and stared up at him. "I don't believe

it." She released him abruptly. "After everything I've done for you?"

"I'll help you find some other land for your horses, but Gary Kidd could not be allowed to win. It was never my intent to hurt you. We can talk some more later, but right now I must find Clair."

David reached out to touch her arm. But Cilla's eyes were flashing dangerously, and she batted his hand away. "Don't bother with me. You haven't helped with anything so far, so run after silly Clair Williams. Her potty little stables mean nothing; it was just a game to me."

Shoving people out of her way, Cilla stormed out.

David struggled in the other direction with his prosthetic and cane, reaching the exit where he'd last seen Clair. He scanned the parking lot anxiously. Was she gone already?

Then he spotted the Jeep. It was half hidden under the trees behind the cottage and there was someone in the driver's seat, arms folded across the top of the steering wheel and head down. His heart contracted. It was Clair.

Could he get to her before she locked the doors against him?

David navigated carefully along the side of the cottage. He opened the passenger door of the Jeep, sprang in quickly, and swung the prosthetic in after him.

Clair sat up and her face was flushed with hot tears. She dashed them away with an impatient hand. "I saw Cilla's face when you won! We trusted you, David. How could you do this to us? It's worse than losing to Gary Kidd."

Her voice broke on a sob. "I can't bear to look at you. Go away and leave me alone."

She reached to start the engine, but David was quicker and pulled the keys from the ignition.

"Give me those!"

He held them away from her in his closed hand. "Clair, please give me a chance to explain."

She grabbed his arm and shook it in fury. "Haven't you humiliated me enough? I came to care for you. I thought we were friends. Then you shelled out two million pounds, just like that, and Cilla lit up like a Roman candle! Did you plan it together? What do I tell everyone now? They know I like you and will think I was involved in this. And all the kids will be devastated."

Clair sobbed, her face in her hands.

David wanted to take her in his arms but knew he must stay well away. "Listen, you remember the day you needed to give me tough feedback and I wanted to go? You said it was important, so I stayed, and you were right. What I want to say is important for us both. Would you listen, just for a few minutes, like I did for you?"

She raised her head and stared at him through red, puffy eyes. "Somehow, Cilla got it wrong. It didn't even cross my mind she'd think I bought the lease for her. We never talked about that and when I left Summerfield, I had no intention of even being here today. But something happened in London, Clair, and I bought the lease for you. I love you. I want to ask if you'll marry me."

Clair's eyes were wide, and she bit her lower lip. What would she say? Probably turn him down, but he had to risk it. David waited.

"It's too much to take in."

He breathed again and went on. "I came back from Afghanistan damaged and angry. You cared, but you also challenged me, and it was just what I needed. All this time, I've been healing and when I left Summerfield after the Nativity performance, I was going back to the Army. But on the way to London, it suddenly hit me. I've changed. I'm different. You are here, but I had left you."

Clair was motionless, listening intently.

So, he went on. "I told you that day in the wood that we had an odd life growing up. Dad gave us money and Mum was in America. She kept in touch and sent loving messages, but there were no hugs or family life at the Manor House. I'm not making excuses, just trying to explain why I'm most at home with the guys in the military."

David felt her relax a little beside him, as if she understood. "Driving away that night, I was with Anthony but felt lonelier than ever in my life before. But I was going back to the only way I knew how to live."

"You went so quickly, there was no time to say goodbye."

David held her gaze. "I couldn't admit I'd fallen for you. I was stubborn and couldn't change my goals at that stage of my life."

She nodded, recognizing a characteristic in them both. "What happened in London?"

"We met up with Mum and Scott; it was busy and sociable–theatre, old friends, and parties. I pretended to be having a great time, but the one person I wanted to see was not there. Late one night, I just couldn't do it anymore and left the party. Ant followed me back to my apartment, to see what was up. We had a few drinks and I told him everything. He said if I truly felt that way, then I had one last chance, and I should take it."

The world outside the Jeep was quiet. Only a

handful of cars were still in the parking lot and Clair seemed to be leaning closer.

David felt a tiny spark of hope. "Anthony helped me raise a massive loan against my apartment. The plan was that, if you won, I could come and talk with you later. But if you didn't, then I would buy the lease for you."

Clair moved now and put her arms around him. Her lips touched his softly and she was crying again. He felt the wetness on his own cheeks and the soft kiss was full of aching relief. He held her close and she clung to him as if to never let go.

"I'm so sorry for the mess. I should have known at the Regimental Dinner. I almost knew in Potlatch Wood, but I pushed it away again. After I talked with Anthony, I went straight out and bought you a promise ring, for if we ever got to this point. May I show you?"

Clair nodded. He handed her the keys to the Jeep and with one arm still around her, felt inside his jacket pocket. Then he opened the little box to reveal a delicate ruby and diamond ring, nestled in black velvet.

"It's not an engagement ring, because you might not want to marry me. But if you accept it, it's my promise that I love you. If you'll have me, I'm going to stick around."

Clair stroked the ring with the tip of one finger. "It's lovely; but what about your job with the military?"

"I went to Regimental HQ, talked with the CO and resigned. I want the chance for us to be together in Summerfield. I love you. Would you accept the ring?"

She smiled and held out her left hand. David slipped the ring onto her engagement finger, raised it to his lips and kissed it. Clair took his hands in hers, the ring sparkling between them.

"I am passionate about what we do here, but after you came back to Summerfield, I found I wanted a love of my own. I wanted you. When you left that day, I thought it was all over for me."

David looked down at their linked hands and his voice trembled a little. "Your work is important. But I want to marry you because of you, and because I need you. Could you love me?"

He had seen that look in her eyes once before, and this time, she didn't shut it down. "I do already. I've loved you from that very first moment in the snow."

She smoothed his face and her eyes were warm brown and shining. "Is it possible we could stay together, through thick and thin? Maybe have a family and grow old together like Granddad and May?"

David felt as if he was saying 'I do' in church — and it was okay. "I'd love that, but before we talk any more, I have a confession."

Clair was immediately tense again.

"No, I'm not lying about loving you. It's just that I bid two million pounds for the lease and have only got a million. Anthony is guarantor for the rest."

She was still for a moment, incredulous, and then began to laugh. "Let me get this straight, David Brown. You mortgaged your only asset, your London apartment, for a million pounds? Then borrowed another million from your brother?"

"Yes, and Anthony's okay with that. But you and the Stables team have a million. Could we put the two funds together and make it work, without him involved?"

"Like a business partnership?"

"Yes, but if you'd marry me, a life partnership as well. We'd be Mr. and Mrs. David Brown, or you could stay as Clair Williams; your choice."

"But I'd be the Captain in the business?"

David chuckled. "Yes. I understand chains of command and you are the Commanding Officer at Summerfield Stables. I'd be the newest recruit on your management team."

Clair was smiling and put her arms around his neck to kiss him again.

"Then I've thought about it enough and my answer is yes, to marrying you. A thousand times yes! But I don't think I could be happy in the same house as your sister. Must we live at the Manor House?"

David held her tenderly, so relieved it was okay, and she was still with him. "Do you think, if we asked nicely, Ted might let us live at Stables Cottage with him?"

Clair's face widened in a grin. "I think he'd love it! Let's go and ask him. He'll have heard what happened at the auction and they'll be waiting to see what state I'm in."

David grinned as he opened the passenger door. "Okay, but promise you'll protect me? I might be lynched before I can ask Ted for your hand in marriage."

Chapter 25

"Would you like to see May's wedding dress?"

"Granddad! You still have it? Why didn't you tell me? I've only seen it in photos. Why didn't Grandma show me? Might it fit? Could I wear it? But even if it fit, it might be in poor condition. Oh, I can't wait to see it!

It was Sunday morning and they were meeting David for lunch at the Potlatch. Clair did not want him to see the dress, just in case, so she called Robert and luckily, he was free. With Ted's instructions of where to find the small trunk, he carried it from the attic to Clair's bedroom.

"Top secret?" she pleaded.

"My lips are sealed." He grinned and left them to it.

Clair knelt on the rug and cleaned the dust off

with a cloth. The old-style traveling trunk was bound with leather straps and had the initials M.W. painted in white on the lid.

"Yes, that's her trunk," Ted sat close on a chair and her heart was fluttering. She reached up to squeeze his hand and then, under the straps, was astonished to find a thick rim of sealing wax all the way around the lid.

"Look at that!"

Ted was surprised too. "May always was an organizer. She made it airtight for you."

Clair broke the seal and opened the lid. There was a waterproof garment bag inside carefully folded and she lifted it out. Laying it flat on her bed, she opened the carefully wrapped froth of lavender tissue paper, to reveal the exquisite wedding dress. She and Ted both had tears in their eyes looking at it.

"May looked so beautiful on our wedding day. She told you about her dad. He was His Lordship's gamekeeper and didn't come back from the First World War. The Duchess had sons, but no daughters and she was very fond of May. The dress was made for her, and that's when the Duke gave us the lease as a wedding gift. He walked May down the aisle at St. Peter's, because her dad had died for his country."

Clair had looked at the wedding photos many

times and May's eyes had shone when she spoke of their wonderful day. She had loved the dress and seeing it now, Clair could see why it was so special. Cut like a Victorian riding costume, it was made of ivory silk, closed modestly to the neck. It had a little jacket with a standup collar and everywhere was edged in lavender silk. Tiny pearl buttons closed the dress all down the back and from elbow to wrist on the long sleeves.

She touched it gently. "It even has a train that loops up onto this button. Oh, it's stunning! Grandma packed it away so carefully and I'd love to marry David wearing it. But do you think she'd have wanted that? Or is it too precious? Maybe it should be in a vintage fashion collection, with her name next to it and the date of your wedding?"

Ted shook his head. "May would be overjoyed you wanted to wear it. She loved you so much, but she was superstitious, as you know. She wouldn't show it to you, because there was no suitable young man in the picture. But she knew David and thought him a fine young man. I think she'd be pleased you might marry him wearing her dress."

* * *

Later, after lunch with David, Clair called Patricia and she came over to see the dress.

Clair put it on carefully. "It was full-length on Grandma, but it's ballerina-length on me and it doesn't quite meet at the back."

Patricia sat nearby and smiled at her in the long mirror. "It's a beautiful dress. I know an expert seamstress in Oxford who works for the English National Ballet. I bet she can make it fit without spoiling it. It's unique, and you have a special glow wearing it."

Clair hugged the delicious secret of the dress close to her heart. But next day, she found her grandfather had hinted something to David.

"For our wedding. Anthony, Ted, and I will be wearing pale grey Victorian tailcoats, pin-striped pants, with grey top hats."

"That sounds fantastic–and I'll enjoy teasing Granddad about the top hat!"

* * *

Patricia drove to Oxford, the dress concealed in a modern garment bag on the back seat of her car. She had completed her short training course to be a verger and she was looking forward to starting her new job the following day.

Clair settled more comfortably in the passenger seat and gazed out of the window at the familiar countryside passing by.

"It's so lovely to relax and be driven. I look forward to taking you out to lunch, after we've seen the dressmaker. I also wanted to tell you about David and I seeing the Reverend Tim. We can be married at St. Peter's, like Ted and May, because it's also the Bartlett-Brown family church. Most of their ancestors are buried in the crypt and we are wondering… " Clair grinned sideways at her, "whether the new verger would help us to arrange the wedding?"

Patricia's face lit up, "Oh, yes!" She immediately pulled over into a turnout. "I didn't like to mention it but was hoping so much you'd ask me. Imagine … my first wedding, and it will be for you and David!"

She applied the brake, switched off the engine and retrieved a tablet computer from her bag. "Do you have a date?

* * *

At the Stables, things had settled down again after the auction.

Sid and David sorted the financials with Anthony and created the business partnership. Everyone on the team was delighted that Robert and Steph were staying on and they began to plan a program with Jack for veteran amputees.

Ted decided not to speak to Gary Kidd about the fence but commissioned a local company to erect a solid barrier between the marshy area and their field. Bonnie could no longer see the juicy grass, and the mud would grow green again in time. One afternoon, all the heavy machinery disappeared, along with Gary Kidd and Kyle Sanders.

Clair laughed when Steph came in from the village to tell her. "Guess what? Kyle's joined Gary in the chicken business and moved to Banbury."

"Yay! Those two deserve each other!"

Cilla had left for California straight after the auction. David stayed on at the Manor House with Mrs. Jessop and began his training with Robert in the yard. Every second day he and Clair rode out together and most evenings were spent happily with Ted, planning the remodeling of the cottage. David took over most of the cooking at Stables cottage, for which they were all truly thankful!

Replies were pouring in from the wedding invitations and David looked up from his emails. "Mum and Scott are coming, but there's nothing from Cilla yet. I've called and emailed, but she's blocked me. Maybe Mum can persuade her to come?"

Clair was secretly relieved to hear that Cilla would not be there. Then David laughed, "Dad's companion has written a 'thank you' for him from the yacht. Apparently, he's too tired to fly anywhere now. It's more likely he's too busy with his own romance! She's his fourth caregiver in two years and younger than Cilla."

"But, didn't you say he was eighty?"

"Yep, but feisty with it. Ant will need to go and sort him out again. He casually mentions marriage to his caregivers and strings them along. But he's invited us to visit him on our honeymoon."

"Maybe . . . if you really want to. But we won't be going anywhere, for it won't be for ages, will it? We need to get the new 'Riding with Challenges' up and running."

* * *

Lizzie and Steph were to be Clair's Matrons of Honor. After several appointments with Patricia's lovely dressmaker friend, May's wedding dress now fit Clair perfectly. She loved it.

Lizzie flew from Edinburgh and stayed with Viv, so she could visit her mum at the care home. Then she met Clair and Steph at Oxford's vintage boutique. Clair had searched online but not found suitable shoes. Here, at last, she found ivory shoes and silk stockings to complete her outfit.

She looked down at them and wriggled her toes. "These are the right period and comfortable. I couldn't wear Grandma's wedding shoes. My feet are three sizes bigger than hers!"

She hugged Steph and Lizzie when they chose lovely dresses, each suited to their own style, but in colors that complemented her gown.

"Oh, it's SO nice to be doing this, after all the tough times of the past months."

"Yeah, but we made it, didn't we?" Steph was jubilant.

"While I am over the moon at the prospect of having my hair styled at your swanky salon!"

Lizzie grinned. "Let alone being at the marriage of Clair Williams to David Bartlett-Brown! Looking back to when we were teenagers, who would ever have thought it?"

* * *

Spring came early to Summerfield for their Easter wedding.

The days grew longer and beech trees in Potlatch Wood sprouted tiny leaves of transparent green. The land was soft with fields of sprouting and the ponies were skittish, kicking up their heels in the new grass.

Clair was unbelievably happy — until three days before the wedding, when it started raining. She was frantic the night before, when Lizzie and Harry arrived.

"Three days, non-stop, I can't believe it!"

Ted greeted them with hugs. "Don't worry, it'll be a beautiful day tomorrow."

Harry had a great respect for country lore and followed him into to the kitchen. "Can you tell that by the wind or something, Ted?"

"Nah, I heard it on the radio this morning."

As predicted, the following day dawned with sunshine in a clear, blue sky. Crocuses and daffodils were blooming in the garden as Lizzie and Steph waited with Clair, ready to go to St. Peter's. They wore pretty circlets of May's lavender in their hair and carried posies of spring flowers. A blackbird 'chip-chip-chipped' as Ted opened the front door to Robert and Nick, turning the pony cart in front of the cottage.

They wore matched uniforms with green top hats and the seats were covered in green throws. Bonnie's mane had been threaded with green and yellow ribbons. Nick grinned down at his mum and

Ted's eyes were misty as he gave Clair his hand into the pony cart.

Then Jack pulled up behind them in his car, wearing Regimental uniform, to chauffeur Steph and Lizzie to the church. But first, he was needed to heave Ted up into the pony cart and Nick could not hold back his peal of laughter.

Ted shook his fist in mock anger. "Young rascal! I may have trouble getting up, but I can get down okay."

Jack drove off with Steph and Lizzie. Bonnie walked steadily up the lane and Ted held Clair's hand, "You look beautiful dear. May and your parents would have been so proud. But I've got the happy job of escorting you today and I'm so pleased you'll be living at the cottage; I couldn't bear to lose you."

The bells of St. Peter's had been silent for two years but now they rang out as the pony cart passed the Saturday market.

People waved and called greetings as Bonnie trotted down the driveway from the village center to the church.

Lizzie and Steph waited under pink flowering cherry trees at the gate and a soft breeze scattered the petals. Clair took Ted's arm. They went quietly to the family grave and stood for a few minutes, each with their own thoughts.

Then they walked back to Patricia, wearing her black verger's robe and she smiled to see them. At her signal, the bells were still, and the organ played a lovely Bach Cantata as Clair and Ted entered St. Peter's.

The church was cool and dark after the bright sunshine. Everywhere was decorated with daffodils, and the church was packed with the smiling faces of their friends.

With her beloved Granddad, Clair walked slowly down the central aisle, through the patterns of jeweled color cast by sunshine through stained glass. Then she saw Cilla.

But her eyes went past, to David, waiting with Anthony and the minister. With a smile that filled her heart, he received her hand from Ted. He seemed too choked with emotion to say anything, but Clair saw the depth of love in his eyes.

The Service and their Vows were traditional and solemn. She prayed they would find contentment in this marriage, for the whole of their lives. Then, Jossie, the Ring Bearer, was released from Jack's car. He bounded in, newly bathed, with an enormous lavender bow tied around his neck. He was so delighted to see everyone that David had to grab him for Anthony to retrieve the rings from his collar!

And then they were married.

Jack stepped forward, ceremonial sword raised in front and he led them from the church. Outside, four friends from the Regiment, two in wheelchairs, held bamboo arches covered in flowers as David and Clair walked beneath.

David shook hands with them all. "Thanks, guys, it means a lot to me that you came today."

Everyone followed them out of the church for joyful photos amid the cherry blossoms, then they set off for the reception at the Stables.

Ted waved as he left with Lizzie and Harry. "See you soon!"

Clair and David walked together to place her bouquet with the loved ones who could not be with them.

Clair whispered, "Thank you for the beautiful dress, Grandma."

Then it was back to their pony chariot, now sporting a 'Just Married' sign! Robert and Nick took Bonnie at a lively trot through the village, slowing to a walk as they turned into the lane.

At the Stables, David helped Clair down and gave Nick a crisp new twenty-pound note. "Thank you, driver, for bringing us safely home."

Nick's face was a picture. He turned to pass the money to Robert, who shook his head. "That's yours, you did most of the driving today."

Hand in hand, Clair and David went in to greet their guests. Everyone had glasses of champagne or sparkling apple juice and waited in the Training Room, around a magnificent three-tier wedding cake. Mrs. Jessop had made it, delighted to have all the family together again. She was catering a grand dinner for them that evening, but this afternoon's reception was for everyone Clair and David loved. All the humans and canines were there, with treats for horses and ponies later.

David was immediately grabbed by some Army guys congratulating him and shaking his hand. Clair saw Cilla standing to one side with Nancy, her and David's mother and went straight over.

"Thank you so much for coming. What a fabulous day; we've been so lucky with the weather! Cilla, I hope we can be better friends now. You're welcome to use the arena for dressage."

Cilla's face softened a little. "Thanks, but I've sold my horses to Zara. I have a job, with a racing stables in Del Mar and I'm staying on in California. Good luck with everything here and look after David for me."

"I will."

David joined them to hug his mum and Cilla. Then he placed a glass of champagne in Clair's hand and steered her to the front.

"You first, Captain."

His arm warmly around her waist, Clair raised her glass to their guests. "Thank you all for your love and support, in good times and bad. I can't quite believe it – but David and I are married, and this is a new start for the Summerfield Stables."

David touched his glass to hers and they sipped champagne before he spoke. David was the man Clair loved. His face was the one she remembered, the kind boy in the snow. Now, he held her hand and turned to their guests.

"I fell in love with Clair when she was teaching me, and I bid for the lease because I wanted to marry her. I've been in combat and awarded medals. But these past few months have shown me that many of the real heroes are here. Where in the world could we be happy, if Summerfield Stables was lost and her heart was broken?"

There was applause and Clair smiled up at him. He turned to her, "Clair, you are my best friend. There is no one I want to travel the future with but you."

Everyone clapped and cheered, then Ted stepped forward. "I want to show you all the first of my wedding gifts."

He led the way outside. They'd been forbidden to go near the covered signboard all week, but now Ted took off the sheet.

Welcome to Summerfield Stables
Partners: Clair Williams and David Brown

They pulled him into a hug with them. Clair thought in that moment, that one was still a perfect number. But if you were lucky enough to find another special one, then it added up to more than two.

Enjoyed this book?

Thanks for joining Clair and David
in Summerfield Village.

If you enjoyed the book, a review would be much
appreciated as it helps other readers discover the
story.

More from Penny Appleton

Love, Second Time Around
- Maggie and Greg's story

Love Will Find a Way
- Jenna and Dan's story

Love, Home at Last
- Lizzie and Harry's story

Love at the Summerfield Stables
- Clair and David's story

Available now:

Love, Second Time Around

Have you read Maggie and Greg's story?

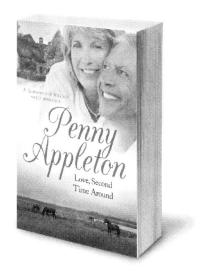

Maggie Stewart is a retired environmentalist, working to preserve the heritage of her little English cottage in Summerfield village. Her children have grown and she's content to ride horses in the countryside and enjoy her retirement.

Except she needs money for her renovations – and she's lonely.

When she joins her old environmental team to go up against an oil company intent on destroying a pristine Scottish river, Maggie finds herself working in opposition to a man she once loved from afar, many years ago.

Idaho ranch owner Greg Warren is rich and entitled, with a dark past that he hides behind a professional smile. But inside, he struggles with loneliness after the loss of his wife and the rage of a wild daughter who won't let him move on.

Love blooms as Maggie and Greg take a chance on a new start, but can they find a balance between the two worlds they inhabit?

In this sweet romance, set between the English countryside and the wide expanse of the Idaho plains, can Maggie and Greg find love second time around?

Available now in ebook,
print, and Large Print formats.

Available now:

Love Will
Find A Way

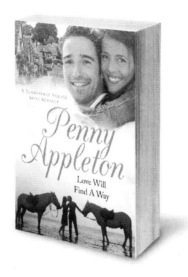

Jenna Warren is an Idaho ranch girl who loves her Appaloosa horse, Blue, and the freedom she has to live her life the way she wants to. But she's increasingly aware that she has never really seen the world, let alone experienced real love, and she hasn't found her purpose.

Daniel Martin is a British schoolteacher, bound by duty to a desperate family situation, and struggling to find his own path as a musician.

When Jenna and Dan meet at a family wedding, they are instantly attracted to each other, but Dan has to leave for Britain the next day. As Jenna follows him back to Summerfield village, a family conflict ignites, tearing their new love apart.

In this sweet romance, set between Idaho and the English countryside, in Japan and tropical Australia, can Jenna and Dan's love find a way through the obstacles that keep them apart?

Available now in ebook,
print, and Large Print formats.

Available now:
Love, Home
At Last

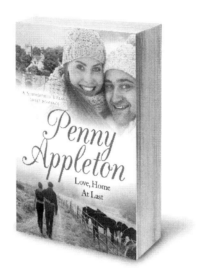

She's an emerging artist. He's a traveling photographer. When new feelings develop, can true love draw them together?

Lizzie "Mouse" Martin is tired of living in the margins. A troubled childhood and years caring for her ailing mother put her art dreams on hold. When Lizzie loses the family farm, she summons her courage, packs her suitcase, and begins a new life in Edinburgh, Scotland. Her brother's best friend is hiring… and he still holds the keys to her heart.

Harry Stewart always thought of Lizzie as a little sister. But between overseas photography excursions, Harry glimpses her transformation from timid farm girl to up-and-coming artist. And he can't help but wonder if their friendship could turn into something much, much more…

When tragedy strikes and a once-in-a-lifetime opportunity emerges, Lizzie must make an impossible choice: stay with the man she's loved all her life or go for the dreams she never thought were possible.

Love, Home at Last is the third standalone book in the charming Summerfield Village Sweet Romance series.

If you like the English countryside and the city of Edinburgh, strong-willed heroines, and emotional journeys of self-discovery, then you'll love Penny Appleton's clean and wholesome love story.

Available now in ebook,
print, and Large Print formats.

About Penny Appleton

Penny Appleton is the pen name of Jacqui Penn, a writer from the south-west of England.

Before she retired, Jacqui travelled in many countries and now enjoys visiting exciting places on vacation. She has been a volunteer for several organizations, including riding experiences for the disabled which features in Love at Summerfield Stables. Many of her stories contain aspects of her adventures and experiences.

Jacqui enjoys life and relishes variety. She loves walking in nature and the city, visiting National Trust properties and museums. She is an avid reader and is interested in wellness, yoga, and good nutrition.

Relationships, animals, and love, in all its myriad forms, are at the heart of her books.

Her favorite authors include Jane Austen, Danielle Steele and Nora Roberts. Also, Deborah Moggach, JoJo Moyes, and Suzanne Collins. Her favorite movies include *Pride and Prejudice*, *Salmon Fishing in the Yemen*, *The Best Exotic Marigold Hotel*, and *Me Before You*.

Acknowledgements

Thanks to my proofreader, Arnetta Jackson, and to Jane at JD Smith Design for the cover design.

Printed in Great Britain
by Amazon

15387506R00166